Next Stop: Nina

by

Robin Raven

Copyright © 2015 Robin Raven

Table of Contents

The Thinking person must oppose all cruel customs, no matter how deeply rooted in tradition and surrounded by a halo. When we have a choice, we must avoid bringing torment and injury into the life of another.

~ Albert Schweitzer

Whoever loved that loved not at first sight?

~ William Shakespeare

Chapter 1~ Wow and Wonder

Art inspired me to rescue myself. I will never forget that moment in the middle of an ordinary week when I discovered something so special that it changed every day that was to follow.

I staggered around the museum, trying to get over how alarmed and on edge I felt. I chose to wander off despite what the consequences would be. I just had to be alone for a bit to take in the pretty art. When I got close to the paintings, it felt as though I was able to step into the majestic worlds depicted in them for a magic, fleeting moment.

The beauty helped me forget about my morning for a while. Before Dad and I got out of the car to join my class on the field trip, he smacked me across the face. It happened as I was pulling the handle on the car door, and the force of his slap made me lose my balance and fall out of the passenger's side onto the concrete.

I didn't scream or make a fuss; I knew better than to draw attention to myself. If anyone asked, I would just say that I fell; I was used to being considered clumsy. The fact that I was a graceful dancer was something people conveniently and quickly ignored.

I felt I deserved to be hit anyway. After all, I hadn't been able to answer the true or false question Dad asked. He was always quizzing me, and I usually got the answers right. I was hoping that he'd stop that sort of stuff when I turned nine years old, or maybe I'd get smart enough to learn how to stop his anger altogether. That had been wishful thinking.

My knees hurt from the fall, and my face still felt hollow and achy from the slap. Still, though, I enjoyed the beautiful, enormous paintings.

I entered a small room that was rather dark except for the soft glow from a spotlight on each painting. I spread my arms and twirled around. How freeing to be in a room that was so filled with beauty.

Suddenly one of the paintings caught my eye for the first time, and I stopped spinning to slowly approach it. This painting was the most beautiful thing I'd ever seen. The colors I noticed immediately were lavender, mint cream green, and turquoise. The textures seemed velvety, as though, if I reached out, the painting would be soft to the touch.

The lack of obvious lines made each object in the painting seem in movement and in harmony with everything else. It was a depiction of a couple getting married in a colorful forest. I imagined how wonderful that forest would smell and what sounds must be coming from the choir whose mouths were open in song. Nothing on the canvas was as you'd expect it to be in the real world, and I fell madly in love with the work of art and its creator.

I got so close to the painting that my nose touched the glass of the frame. When I finally pulled myself away, I noticed its placard, and I studied it:

Painting: *Autumn Joy*
Artist: Leonard Daley (born England, October 25, 1955)
Date: 1979
Medium: Oil on Canvas
Dimensions: Sheet: 60 × 72 in. (152.4 × 182.9 cm)
Credit Line: On Loan from the Artist

The painting was created about a decade before I saw it. Long after that enchanting moment, I searched through forests and fields. I inspected wildflowers along white sand beaches. I wandered up streams and down near the creek by my house. I tried for years to find just a glimpse of the heart-stirring beauty from Leonard's painting, but it held a special kind of magic that existed only there.

Chapter 2 ~ Lost

I wonder whether I should kill myself or make toast. That's a typical thought that races through my mind. I want to beat my own self up, so I make excuses for why my ex-husband actually did. I left him, though, and chose to save myself.

I just keep asking myself: *Why?*

I flip up my long, blonde hair, but it quickly flows down my back. I sigh because, even if I work on it for hours, it never looks exactly like I imagine it should.

I put on a black bra. The fact that it's black and lacey helps me feel more like a woman who might dare to do the things she dreams about at night. Black bras help me feel a little less like me.

Next, I reach my arms through the red sleeves of my shirt and pull on my rainbow-colored, pleated skirt. I put on red tights and non-leather boots. I laugh as I realize that my outfit is perhaps better suited for a child, but I blew out 37 candles on my last birthday cake. Nevertheless I dress however I like.

As I pull out my glittery, pink make-up case, I get the strange feeling that I'm being watched. I glance around my bedroom, and it's clear that nobody is there. Somehow that doesn't make me feel any better.

I have a hard time shaking this uneasy feeling as I apply glossy lipstick. I open my green eyes wide to put on just a little too much mascara and a slightly uneven stream of eyeliner. No matter how many times I try, I cannot perfect the application of eye make-up. I tend to err on the side of way too much.

I stick my tongue out and make a face in the make-up mirror. I once hated myself so much that I took razorblades to the wrists that I now lovingly caress. I make a current habit of drawing gentle hearts over them with the rollerball of perfume as if to say: *I'm sorry. I really do love you now.*

The truth is that I slashed my wrists and arms just once when I was a senior in high school. I wanted to shut out my bully's harsh words along with my own affirmations of self-hatred that constantly flooded through my brain. The pain was too enormous to be tolerable, so I undressed and lowered myself into a warm bath.

On that weird night, I took a razor and slashed my arms and wrists in at least 30 places. Despite the agony, I hadn't cut myself deeply enough to leave permanent physical scars. In fact, I didn't even need to go to the hospital. When I realized that I had failed miserably at the morbid task at hand, I washed myself off, bandaged the wounds, and continued on like nothing had happened.

Now I just feel a lot of love and sympathy for my younger self. I wish I could explain things to her in the calm, soft, and compassionate way that she needed to hear things. I mostly just want to tell her that it's okay. It was the only thing she knew how to do.

I shake off the memory as I continue getting ready. I look around again, though, as if to make sure that I don't have an audience.

When all is said and done, I force myself to go to the full-length mirror. It's then that I can't forget what I've become. I can lose myself in parts of me. My face isn't so bad. My hands are soft with a perfect manicure. My eyelashes are quite long and thick; they're more than passable. Yet, when I look at who I am as a whole, I see someone who's much different that the pieces I've allowed myself to glimpse so far today.

The full-length mirror reveals what I can't deny. I'm fat now. My reflection shows everything I hate about myself. I wish that my every impulse wasn't to despise how I look. I think of other large women as absolutely beautiful, yet I cannot allow the same objective lens to fall upon me. I can't accept myself today, and I have no vested interest in coping with the truth.

I ask myself: *How did it come to this? How did I get to this point?*

When my ringtone of Madonna's "She's Not Me" starts blaring through my disgusted reverie, I am so startled that I literally jump. I grab the phone to see who it is. My favorite person in the world is calling me, so I toss my cell phone down on my dresser without answering the call. I'm too sad to deal with something so pleasant.

Thoughts of rope, sleeping pills, and jumping off bridges dance through my head, but I try to consider a somehow less selfish way to end things. I'm no George Bailey, and I don't expect everybody in town to come show me love. I may dream of the perfect ending in a favorite movie, but I fear that my pain may be just beginning.

Chapter 3 ~ More to Life

Hope transforms. It's more than a vague concept or a specific feeling. It saves us and inspires us to try for joys that go beyond unfathomable dreams. It's not innocent, though. It's not the good guy. Hope lies and deceives if that's what it takes to keep us going. When something peels back, and the unvarnished truth peeks through the veil that hope provides, the pain can be worse than mere death.

Still, I wouldn't be here without hope. I don't begrudge hope the cruelty that it must take on to complete its mission. Looking at the situation for what it really is, though, makes me realize that I survived just to end it all here and now, so what was the point? It's my darkest moment, and I am now acutely aware that this trauma was too severe for me to ever recover from it.

My first memory is of fiery, unrelenting pain…What I learned from that heightened awareness of suffering was that nobody should ever feel that overwhelmed, helpless, or unloved. Rather than allow the moments of cruelty to form me, I chose who I would be in the aftermath, during the times of quiet, tearful reflection.

Long before I understood much about this rabid world, I felt empathy and respect for all who can feel. Despite the hatred I'd seen, I realized I had to live my life based on love. I decided to live my life as though the world and its people were as they should be, not as I learned some folks could be. I tried to be a blessing to everyone I encountered, but that hadn't been enough. It still wasn't.

I remember feeling powerless over the physical pain of the belt, but what really tortured me was the thought that someone chose to make me feel that way, that my own father wanted to hurt me. The overwhelming convergence of physical, emotional, mental, and spiritual pain brought out a suspicion that everyone who was supposed to care for me didn't. In those young and unknowing moments of pure fear, I felt that even God must hate me.

The belt came crashing down on my four-year-old self as my father wielded it with anger and some kind of weird satisfaction. My second memory is my father jovially bragging about the whipping to visiting family members, speaking with a twisted pride about how he tore me up; they nodded and laughed.

Welcome to the Deep South, kid. Maybe have a nice life, or just consider yourself lucky if you make it out alive.

Making it out alive was the curse, though. I learned to fear authority back then, but I knew instinctively that it was not necessarily worth respecting. Neither was he. He's been gone so long now, and I should have left all these things behind long ago. I can't, though, and he's won.

I thought of all these things during my drive to the hotel and while I checked in. The room smells of salt, mold, and old disinfectant. I think of that news special I saw last week when they showed exactly how filthy the average hotel room is. I don't even want to think how this dive would fare in that test, but I suppose none of that matters now.

The truth is that I love hotels. They feel like escape, old memories that don't belong to me, and a comforting sort of murkiness. With hotels, you can't fathom all the lives who've shared the same space you're in and what all has happened throughout the building before you sauntered in. How many people made love on the mattress, cried on the pillows, or just maybe hid from the world a while?

I catch a glimpse of my reflection in the mirror that's awkwardly placed outside the bathroom. I'm no more accepting of myself than I was when I struggled to get ready this morning. My own image is more repulsive than the stink of the room, yet both are starting to overwhelm me. I wish I could love myself like that Olivia Newton-John song on my iPod tells me to do, but that thought seems utterly ridiculous.

I pull the gun case out of my bag, then put the gun on the end table. I think of how I've made more mistakes in my thirties than I managed to in the whole rest of my life. I survived the abuse of my ex, sure, but who I was inside has been irrevocably changed. I don't feel as though my true self came out the other side of that. It is time to just stop the pain.

A quick succession of knocks on the door interrupts my stoic acceptance, and I start to panic. Tears are rolling down my cheeks before I realize the deep sorrow I've been denying. I can't speak, but finally I grab onto a towel and toss it over the gun.

I slowly go to the door and speak to whoever is knocking in a calm, controlled way.

"Who is it?"

"Housekeeping."

"Oh. I just checked in. I don't need anything. The room is fine."

"I have towels."

"It's okay. I'm fine. No towels. Thank you."

"Okay. Okay. Good night."

I sigh as I imagine all the towels that the poor woman would need tomorrow. I hate myself, but I can't think of another way. Maybe I should accept the towels and try to make it less messy. I rush to the door, throw it open, and step onto the open-air walkway. The maid, a beautiful young woman in her early twenties, turns to me with a forced smile.

"Excuse me. I'm sorry. On second thought, I will take those towels. Thank you. By the way, I'm Nina."

"Nina, you say? Nice to meet ya. I'm Frannie."

Frannie piles about four towels in my outstretched arms, then waves me a quick good night as I thank her. She hurries to the next room and opens it with an old-fashioned key. Most hotels I've stayed in had more high-tech means of entry.

As I enter my room again, my mind wanders. I can't focus. I start pondering how things could possibly be different. It's September 1, 2016. That's what my smartphone says, and it has a tendency to be right too often. That's more than I can say about myself for sure, and I feel a bitter giggle stir in my throat at that silly realization. I glance down at my phone, and only another minute has passed.

Cotard's syndrome is a rare psychotic condition in which someone actually thinks they're dead. They are absolutely certain of it, with no doubts or second thoughts. It was identified as far back as the 19th century. People walk around convinced that they are dead and just killing time before their burial.

I wish I had Cotard's syndrome. That way, I wouldn't have to go through with what brought me to the hotel. I'd already feel dead. That has to feel better than living.

I hate being alive when this is what my life is. I wish I had never been born. I don't say that in a selfish kind of way. Ultimately we are selfish beings when it comes to staying alive or dying, though, and the truth is what it is.

I pick up the towel that I'd used to hide it, and I gaze at the gun on the nightstand; it threatens to take away the worst days of my life. I look away from the bullets beside it, although somehow they comfort me with their cruelty. The mere presence of the semiautomatic makes me a hypocrite, though. I've always loathed guns, yet here I am, turning to one in my lowest, most needy moments.

I quickly put the bullets in the gun the way that the man at the pawn shop showed me. I take in a deep breath. Okay, I'm going to do it. I close my eyes to prepare for the end, then something makes me open them again.

I look up through the hot tears that are now falling uncontrollably from my eyes, and I am completely shocked by what I see. It's a print, a beautiful art print in this ugly hotel. I'd know the print anywhere; I once saw the original in person. It's unmistakably a print of an exquisite, surreal work of art by Leonard Daley. It's the one I saw in that museum so many years ago, the one that saved and inspired me.

I take in a deep breath and find myself putting down the gun. I walk slowly to the work of art. I get up close to it. I stare and gasp at its beauty. Who am I to turn my back on a world where I can admire that kind of art? It reminds me of all the hopes and experiences that make staying on the planet worthwhile.

I take the print of Leonard's painting off the wall and place it on the nightstand by the bed. I lie down while never taking my eyes off the art. I just need to be near it.

One more night, I tell myself. *I can make it through one more night.*

Chapter 4 ~ What You're Living

It seems that, at the exact moment when I fall asleep in the hotel room, I start to wake back up again. I'm no longer comfortable. In fact, feel upright with vinyl beneath my head. My breathing quickens, and I'm suddenly afraid of fully waking up. I sense that something isn't right.

Before I open eyes, I smell burning candles, the sour apple shampoo of little children, and birthday cake. I hear the sound of kids laughing with delight and talking with abandon as the Rock-afire Explosion band plays. My eyes open with a start to find my childhood classmates gathered around the table at Show Biz Pizza Place, the entertainment-saturated eatery that closed down decades ago.

Wait, my childhood classmates? They look like little kids. That can't be. We're having our 20-year reunion next year. None of this can be real. It has to be some sort of vivid dream.

How did I get here? What the hell? Did someone slip me LSD or something stronger, something scarier, yesterday? When did they have the chance? The last person I remember seeing was the maid at the hotel. I try to remember what I ate and drank yesterday, and it was precious little.

The gun was only there for comfort. I chose not to use it. This can't be hell. I didn't really go through with it, did I? I shook my head in answer to my own unspoken question. No, no, no. Could I have done it without remembering it? No, I didn't. Maybe the gun went off somehow anyway. All I know is that it's September 1, 2016, and this can't be happening.

Why am I here? I loved this pizza joint, that's true. I loved it enough to know that all chains of it had closed years ago. I even remember that its commercials said it was the place where everyone can be a kid. I'm pretty sure that didn't pertain to 37-year-old women who suddenly see their old classmates as children before their eyes.

I reach down and feel the body I'm in. It's so tiny. The fat is gone! I look down and see a child's body, and I recognize my old grey dress. I loved it so much that I wore it out. It doesn't even exist now, so how am I wearing it? I scream as I feel my small hands. It's as though someone shrunk me!

I see Mrs. Benedict, Jenny's mom, coming towards me. I force myself to smile up at her when suddenly she starts shaking me.

"Nina Newman," she scolds, "How can you be so selfish? Trying to steal the attention at Jenny's birthday."

Now I know that I must be back in time because there's no way someone in 2016 would dare shake someone else's kid to the point of dizziness without expecting some kind of madness. At least I hope not.

"I'm sorry," I manage to say, "I just feel bad."

"Oh. Why didn't you say so? Well…I'm sorry, too, then. Go lie down on the bench there. I'll go call your mom to come get you."

Right. No cell phones? I watch her rush to the payphone. She looks scared now. She lost control, and her breath stinks of vodka. I never noticed such desperation in any of my friends' parents while I was growing up. Was I totally oblivious? Why am I worrying about her now when clearly something crazy is going on?

I make my way to the bright red bench where she suggested I rest. Lord knows that I don't need to make any more waves. The squeaky bench smells like vinyl and old pizza. I notice that Mrs. Benedict is rushing to me frantically as soon as I lie down.

"Your mom's gonna be here soon, dear" she says, "Here's two rolls of tokens for you to use next time you come here. Look, I'm sorry that you got sick, and I'm sorrier that I got mad. Can we keep that a secret?"

I take the tokens, although I can tell that it's a sort of bribe. I smile at her. I have far bigger problems than ratting her out even if I still feel a bit out of sorts.

"Taking this one to the grave," I say with a laugh.

Oh, she wouldn't get the reference to the *Pretty Little Liars* theme song. The show hasn't even started yet. If they're even born, the Pierces are probably kids themselves out there in this weird universe, or is the world beyond this pizza place even the way it should be?

Like I suspected earlier, this must be a dream. Maybe it'll all fade away soon if I just ride it out.

I can see the front parking lot from my spot on the red bench. I see a pale young boy looking into the pizza place. He can't be more than 15 years old, and he wears an oversized suit and a big frown. He slowly passes right by the front door, and I notice a red-haired woman in a bright, floral jumper who's walking with him. They stop to talk.

I am quickly distracted by the sight of Davey! My big brother is coming through the front door! Mom must have sent him to get me. He's really here! He's alive and smiling! I have to really be back in time if he's not dead. He looks so young and beautiful. As I race towards him at full force, I am half-expecting it to just be a cruel hologram, but he grabs me and lifts me in his arms.

"Davey!" I scream excitedly.

Having a brother who's a decade older than me used to seem unfair, but now it's wonderful. I'll take Davey any way that I can get him. If this is a dream, I hope I never wake up.

"Wow, cool out. Since when are you this excited to see me? This party must be really buggin', huh? I told Mom this morning that the parties here aren't worth it," he scoffs as he puts me back on solid ground. I grab his hand, not ready to let go.

"Where's Mom?"

"She's waiting in the car. Go tell her you're still alive. I'm gonna grab a pizza, and I'll be out in a minute."

I nod. I don't want to argue with him, but it takes me a second too long to let go of his hand. As he rushes off, I slowly walk out to the parking lot. For a second, I had to consider which car we would have at this point. Oh, how I remember that old station wagon!

I see my mom behind the wheel of the light brown car. She looks so different. This is the most beautiful sight I've ever seen. I missed her most of all. I gasp because I see that she still has a specific sort of hope about her. I run to her even faster than I rushed to Davey.

Chapter 5 ~ Home

My room! As soon as we arrive back at the house, I rush to my old bedroom. How I missed it. It felt like I lost a vital part of myself when my room was turned into a home gym after I moved out, and it's wonderful to see all my old posters in their proper place.

How is it that this is exactly my childhood room? I see the beautifully framed print of *Autumn Joy* over my frilly wicker bed. The colors of my bedspread were chosen to match the brilliant colors in the painting. It looks so comfortable that I could cuddle up with my stuffed animals for a nap if I wasn't so shocked.

I see things I've forgotten like the old Lisa Frank stickers on my hope chest. My E.T. and Gizmo toys sit together on a shelf. A blue teddy bear triggers a whole new series of memories. My dad won him for me at a fair. My dad liked playing the hero! Of course he did. How could I have forgotten that about him?

I then notice the necklace on my dresser. Oh, how much I cried when I'd lost it as a teen. Its centerpiece is a turquoise and white topaz pendant, and a string of gemstone beads in a rainbow of colors serves as its chain. I put it on immediately, and I think about why it was so special to me. Davey gave it to me on my ninth birthday in a real, grown-up jewelry box.

Once I fasten it, I remember what it was like to be a little girl with dreams that never stop growing. I pretend a prince is asking me to dance, and I curtsy.

A stifled giggle interrupts me. I stand straight at attention. I thought I was alone in my room, but I notice Davey standing in the doorway. He's studying me. Does he somehow know I've traveled back in time? No, of course not.

"What's with you?" he says.

Although his voice sneers, a kind smile is plastered on his face. I can't help but smile at him. He's really here. How do I stop him from ever taking a drink or getting behind the wheel of a car? For now, he takes me by the hands and twirls me around the room. It's suddenly familiar again. Oh, how often he always did this. He keeps going until I'm too dizzy and have to let go. I sit on the ground as the room seems to spin, and that's half the fun.

"Okay," he says as he kneels to my level. "Listen, Mom's worried. I noticed you were acting kind of weird earlier, but I figured Mom's overreacting like she always does. Then I walk in here, and you're star-ing at your stuff like it's possessed. What the hell happened at Show Biz?"

I laugh because he's acting so beautifully like himself. He always liked to start his sentences with "listen" as if I had any choice in the matter. I throw my arms around him and hold tight because I never want to let him go.

"You're seriously scaring me now. What's with you?"

"Maybe it's the fucking flu," I say, then realize what I've done.

Instead of showing fear, I smile. Davey feigns shock and horror for my benefit, but I know he says that word all the time when he's out with his friends.

"I won't tell on you because I didn't like the way Dad hurt you the last time you said that, but you better watch it. Sick or not, they'll freak out if you start talking like that."

"I so, so appreciate it," I say jokingly, trying to create some kind of renewed bond with him.

A silly smile crosses his face, and he starts to leave the room. He turns back to talk to me, though.

"Come on down to dinner, would ya?"

"Yeah, okay, just give me a few minutes, okay? Please?"

"Please? Who taught you manners?"

I consider how I've longed to have my brother's name roll off my tongue for a long time.

"Wait a second, Davey."

He turns and smiles at me.

"Don't think I'm a total goof, but what's today's date?"

"Uh, Saturday?"

"Okay, but the date?"

"January 7…"

"Of?"

"1989. I know we've only been at it a week now, but haven't you been writing the date all week at school?"

"Yeah. I just…The New Year. It came so fast."

Davey looks at me. He knows for sure that something is off. I want to tell him everything. I want to warn him. Somehow I know that this would be trouble, though. Right? I'll see. Maybe I'll tell him later. I want to tell him how much I've missed him. Maybe he'd keel over from a heart attack, though, and that's if he believed me.

"Look, kiddo. Want me to tell Mom you're not up for dinner?"

I nod my head yes. I want to have dinner with my family, but I have to get a handle on all this.

"Okay then. I'll try to smuggle you up a Coke and some junk food later."

"Thanks, Davey!"

I run to hug him, and he hugs me back for a moment. Then he rushes out of the room.

I close the door behind him and turn the lock just to be on the safe side. That's when I notice the record player. I pick up what I remember as one of my favorite 45s. I had taken it from my mom's collection, but she never mentioned that she was missing it. "We've Only Just Begun" by The Carpenters always soothes me.

I put it on the turntable. The lovely sound of the needle on spinning vinyl fills the short distance between me and the record player. I start to dance around the room as I'd done when I was younger. My short legs feel even shorter.

This has to be a dream. The more I think about it, the more convinced I am, but when do dreams go on this long? Could God be sending me back in time for a reason? I'd been a Christian all my life until I found myself trapped in abusive situation as an adult, too, then I'd just given in and let all doubts take over. I'd lost my faith. I wanted to change, but not this way. Somehow this doesn't feel like a spiritual expedition.

I look down at the celebrity magazine in my room. I must have taken it from Davey's collection. This month's issue proudly proclaims it to be a "Special Future Issue" in a large square in the center of the magazine. How is it that my future seems to be the past?

The reason why I took this particular issue quickly becomes clear. When I thumb through the magazine, I come across an interview of Leonard Daley. His painting had saved me at the hotel, hadn't it? I'd clung to it just as fiercely as a child when I first discovered it. When I first found this interview of him, I remember reading it over and over again.

I look at the small photo of handsome Leonard in the magazine. In fact, I find myself unable to stop staring at his captivating eyes and dark, styled hair. He looks so at ease in the picture, and I wonder what the people around him were saying and doing. Were they catering to his every need? Was he talking to a crew member, or perhaps a model was flirting with him on her way to another photo shoot for the magazine. Photographs never tell me enough about a situation to satisfy my curiosity.

As I read the interview of Leonard, I get a little dizzy. I forgot how compassionate and caring he revealed himself to be in the article. How does one manage to convey that through the pages of a magazine? I don't even know.

When I peel myself away from the escape that the interview provides, the enormous weight of this new reality hits me. How am I supposed to handle being back at the scene of the crime before it's happened?

Chapter 6 ~ Sunday Morning

I start to stir in bed, and I am afraid to open my eyes. I feel so much better, though. I inhale, and I know instantly that the air in my lungs can't possibly be the stale air of the cheap motel. I'm still here. I've somehow traveled back in time. This is for real.

"Time to wake up!"

I hear my mother's voice and suddenly realize why I woke up. I open my eyes and see that she's standing at the doorway calling me to breakfast. My mother! For the second time within the space of a few seconds, it sinks in all over again that I'm really back in time

I blink a few times, and I freeze in renewed shock. A horror sweeps over me, yet I scream in delight. I'm waking up to live my first full day back in this seemingly old world where I am once again ten years old.

"Nina! Nina! What is the matter with you? Are you okay? Hugh! Get in here!"

"No, no, I'm okay!" I say as I force myself to stop screaming.

"Okay? You're okay? You look like you're in shock."

I take deep breaths as my mother comes to sit beside me. She drapes her arms around me. I take deep breaths and stare as my father and brother file into the room. My entire family is here with me in this moment. It occurs to me that my parents aren't much older than me. I'm acutely aware of being in my late thirties, and so are they.

I manage to convince them that I'm alright, then we all make our way into the kitchen for breakfast.

"Have some bacon," my mom says cheerfully as she sits a big platter of it on the table.

"Oh, God, no."

Oops, a reflexive reaction on my part, and I worry about what her response will be.

"Nina Susannah, did you just take the Lord's name in vain?"

"No, Mama, I was just kidding…It's just…I'm a vegan now."

"What's that? From *Star Trek*?"

Oh, right. Nobody talked about being vegan in my town in the 1980's.

"I just don't eat bacon, okay? I'm sorry. Can we just have fun this morning?"

"Fun? Fine. You don't have to eat bacon. Have whatever you want. I'm just glad you're feeling better"

"Can I ask for one more favor?"

I know that I should have a bit more fear. I know how unhinged Dad can be at the mere mention of something that may not go his way. I have to take chances, though, if I am ever going to get any of this figured out.

"Let's hear it. What do you want?" Davey asks with a grin on his face.

"I don't feel so good. Can I stay home from church?"

As soon as I ask for this favor, I notice Dad's gaze from across the table.

"What the matter?" he asks.

"I got sick at the pizza party last night, and I just don't feel all that well yet."

"All that well? You sure are talking funny," scoffs Davey.

"Fine. Stay home, if David will stay with you," Dad concludes.

"I think I can sacrifice a sermon with Pastor Plumb for my little sis," Davey says.

Man, he is milking this situation! I happen to remember how he loathed going to church. We smile at each other when we think our parents aren't looking.

"That settles it!" Mom declares. "You two stay here. If you go outside, no further than around the block. Deal?"

We both nod in agreement. If Davey is anything like I remember him, though, he will not bother to watch me. His idea of babysitting is plying me with junk food and letting me do whatever I want as long as I don't cause him any trouble. That's just part of why I love it when he's my babysitter.

Chapter 7 ~ Where There's Smoke

I try to stay calm. Almost 24 hours have passed since I came into this seemingly old, yet somehow new, existence. I want to know all the answers, but I'm jaded enough to know that they probably won't be easy to come by. That doesn't mean that I can resist at least searching for clues, though.

I go to grab my purse before I leave the house, but I am reminded that I no longer have a wallet or a proper identity. What if I forget who I am? I feel like life itself could slip from my fingers. Is this the punishment for suicide?

I remember the woman who wore all black at my father's funeral; I think of how she came up to me and whispered, "Your father's burning in hell right now, and that's where he'll always be. Never let anyone tell you otherwise."

That's a hell of a thing to tell a kid, but maybe she was right. Maybe she joined him when all was said and done. Maybe that's where I'll go, too.

I try to dismiss these thoughts as I walk along the neighborhood in my jelly shoes. I look down and marvel at my tiny feet. Not that they ever got much bigger! My feet feel weird just the same. Everything feels weird and like it doesn't quite fit. I almost stumble because I'm still not used to this new-again body, but I catch myself on a white picket fence.

"Excuse me!"

A shrill voice scares me so badly that I finally do lose my balance, and I fall flat on my ass. I look up and see a young woman holding out her hand to me as she tries to stifle her laughter. I grab it as she pulls me to my feet and starts to talk my ear off.

"I'm sorry," she says, "I didn't mean to scare you. I thought you were messing with our fence. Some rascals stole boards right off it last week. I can tell, though, that the bandit couldn't have been you. Look, I'm sorry, you hear? I'm Maddie Jenkins."

I look at her, trying to remember if I knew her before. I can't remember any of my adult neighbors from childhood, and I certainly don't remember her. She is barely an adult, though; she looks like she's in her late teens. She wears a striped shirt with a floral skirt, yet her headband matches the skirt perfectly.

"I'm Nina," I hear myself say.

"Well, Nina, will ya accept a cup of hot cocoa as an apology? If it comes with a few chocolate chip cookies? I'll serve it over there! You can play on the swing while I go get them."

Maddie points to a beautiful corner of her yard where two tire swings hang from different trees. There's a wooden, rustic table in the middle of them. I nod to signal my acceptance and rush over to start swinging on one of the tire swings.

I'm feeling a little like I remember a child should feel. This is really nice. As I swing higher, I find myself looking into one of the windows because I see a face peeping up out of the window. The little girl must be only three or so.

I know I'll never forget the child's bright blue eyes and the way that they express themselves with what looks like an adult awareness. I then chide myself for letting my imagination run wild. Do I really expect to find other time travelers in this weird reality I'm facing? I have reached no conclusions about what the heck is happening to me.

Chapter 8 ~ A Day in the Life

I wake up to the artificial, somehow cutesy sound of the train alarm clock going off. It chug-a-lugs in a small circle, and it sounds like the fun times I've enjoyed with Mom. We always longed to travel and did so as often as we possibly could. We were never afraid of taking chances if it meant having a good time and enjoying whatever we could grab from life.

Today will be my first school morning as an adult in a child's body. I can't begin to imagine how I'm going to be able to cope throughout my day. As difficult as it is to be a grown-up with its crushing responsibilities, it's even harder to be a kid with so much uncertainty stretching out for the rest of your life.

I like to think that I stand on my own. I want to envision myself as truly free. I don't want the obligations of being dependent, and I needn't dream up a version of myself with a man to feel whole. However, back in my child body, I feel like I'm not a woman at all any more, and I realize that I've taken a strong sense of satisfaction in what power my body may hold as a woman.

I look around my bedroom, and I suddenly feel a sense of total joy. I have my childhood bedroom back! I hadn't exactly been happy in here in my first life, but now I can be. Why not? What else is there to do? I seem to be stuck here. Wouldn't a lot of people want to go back to being 10 years old again?

The thing is, I cannot lose sight of the fact that, in my first and original lifetime, my dad threatened to kill us all. In the end, he murdered Mom and Davey before offing himself. That was far worse than if he'd gotten me. I loved Mom and Davey more than anything.

If I'm going to prevent my dad from going off the deep end in this lifetime, I have to prevent the downward spiral of events that led to his breakdown. I try to think of it like that, in the most clinical terms I can muster, to prevent constant emotional meltdowns that help no one.

I tried to figure out where it all went so wrong many times, and I never had a definite answer. I did have my theories, though. I knew things started to rapidly accelerate in a downward spiral when my brother got in that drunk driving accident. So my first plan is to help Davey while also trying to placate Dad. .

Things are hopping as I walk down to get some breakfast. Dad is at the breakfast table, and I sit down beside him. I wait patiently for him to eventually put down his newspaper and give me his undivided attention for a minute or two.

"Can I go to work with you this weekend, Daddy?" I ask.

He looks at me. I see surprise in his eyes. I wasn't close to him before, so I assume I haven't been close to him in this weird awakening.

"Why?" he asks.

"I just think it would be fun."

"I reckon," he replies and goes back to reading his newspaper. "It's only Monday. The weekend's a long way off."

Feeling satisfied with the hope that I can make progress with Daddy, I continue on my day. This whole kid thing can't be that bad. How leisurely will my life be if I can ace all these elementary subjects?

I asked to wait for the school bus. In my old life, I relied on my mom to drive me to school every day, but I decide that I need to branch out a little. I suddenly long to keep experiencing new things, even though the ability to completely relive the past is within my grasp.

I've never really fit in among people my own age. I generally preferred the company of older people from as early as I can remember.

The bus stops in front me, and I feel like a misfit as I ascend the steps. It gets even worse when I step on the bus, and nobody invites me to sit with them.

I notice some children shuffling their backpacks and books, spreading them around on the seats, so there's no longer enough room to sit beside them. Now that these kids are so much younger than I am in terms of years I've lived, they're not really threatening to me. I don't actually care that I have nowhere to sit.

"That's *my* seat," I hear a voice squeak as soon as I sit down in the first row of empty seats on the bus, and I recognize it as belonging to a kid named Rita.

"But you were sitting two rows back. Nobody was here," I argue like I never would have as a real little kid.

"I had to tell Julie a secret. I'm ready for my seat back now," she exclaims.

"Tough, because it's mine now. You're welcome to sit beside me if you want, though."

The truth is that I don't know whether Rita is telling the truth or not. When I was really little, she always treated me like I was some subpar human being beneath her snotty little nose. Although I used to worry about what she thought and said about me, I no longer give a single shit about what she says or does any more.

I stay in the seat more to prove a point to this little brat than for any other reason. I begin to have second thoughts as tears well up in her big, brown eyes, and she screams for the bus driver.

"What's goin' on back there? Don't make me get involved. You girls make me get involved, and I'm going to have to report this to the principal. I suggest you solve this real quick. You have one minute," bellows the bus driver.

Rita looks at me with rage and what seems to be fake tears.

"You'll regret this!" she hisses before rushing down the aisle to another open seat.

I think: *Actually, Rita, regret is a word you won't throw around when you know what it's like to have one.*

I soon arrive at school, and I groan at the realization that I have P.E. first period. At this school, as I remember all too well, they even make the little kids change clothes for gym class.

I look at the lockers. Just the sight of them makes a gnawing panic rise in my chest. Why did grown-ups put kids through such useless torture? Having sweaty gym clothes all piled in metal lockers seems pointless. Fourth graders should still be on the playground, not feigning a miniature version of "Carrie" in the locker room.

Aside from that frustration, I am getting used to my shorter-than-usual legs, and, contrary to how I felt in the morning, it feels great not to have breasts. I enjoyed them a little less than I realized.

Chapter 9 ~ Moonrise

Moonrise and moonset are terms that I never heard in my old life. At least I don't think I did. I heard them on television earlier. I'm struggling to discern whether some things are happening for the first time in this new existence or whether they're just new to me because I've forgotten some of the more mundane things about my past.

I try to concentrate on lighter subjects, but I am anxious and frustrated. I have an anger that lives in me. Of course it goes away some of the time, but it tends to keep a permanent address somewhere within me. I've seen too much horror and injustice to ever send it away on a permanent vacation. It doesn't rule my life, and I don't think of it most of the time, though.

I am attempting to spend more time with my dad, so I do accompany him to his job. I love every minute of it. I sit in the office reading a book and occasionally making copies or bringing Dad a file. Meanwhile, I try to observe everything I can about what is going on with him; I must uncover some of the secrets that sent him over the edge, making him want to kill me and my family.

At lunchtime, I still have no answers, but I eagerly go to the door to pay the pizza delivery man. I tip the young boy 40 percent of the bill, which is only two dollars. As a former waitress in my old life, I cannot resist the temptation to give what I consider fair tips any time I receive a service. I wasn't thinking about how cheap Dad was, though.

I bring the pizza to Dad's desk, where we've decided to have lunch, and I give him the change.

"What are you, a thief? Where's the rest of the money?" Dad asks as he counts it again.

"Oh, that's the only change. I gave the guy two dollars for a tip," I explain.

"What? You liar. Where is it?"

"The deliveryman works hard. It's hot out, and he looked so tired…"

I try to justify my choice, but it's no use. I can see that Dad wishes the walls weren't so thin. He looks out the open door of his office. He sees that people are close by and would easily hear me getting my punishment then and there. I know this because that's what he says to me through clinched teeth as he counts the money once again.

As the day goes by, Dad seems to calm down, though. I am thrilled to see that he is in an especially good mood when he gets off work at five o'clock. It's Saturday night, and Dad's off for two days now. He stops by the convenience store and gets me a frozen drink on the way home. Some of my anger subsides as I try to live in the moment.

"I love you and your million dollar freckles," my dad says as he drives into our neighborhood.

I feel warm and complete. Somehow, I forget that I'm not really a child, and the approval of my dad means everything in that moment.

I think: *Oh my gosh, I do love you.*

I want to tell my dad loudly and proudly that I love him, but don't dare. I loved my father? How could I forget that, in spite of all the crap he always did, I once loved the cold, cruel man that he was. This makes me very uncomfortable. I wiggle and adjust my seatbelt.

Can I really do it all over again? Could it be that I just had a dream, and that horror of adulthood never really happened? Maybe it was an angel who was sent down to warn me of a possible future, I reason.

Chapter 10 ~ Corner of My Mind

The joy I find in the relationship with Dad is entirely too short-lived. I fear that he is slowly becoming unstable once again. The calendar shows me that it is going to be Valentine's Day in less than a week. I've been back in time for over a month now, and things seem to be going where they went in my first awareness of life.

I get the creeps when I walk in the den. I look around, and it's terrifying. Nearly every time I hang out there, I get horrified all over again. It hasn't gotten any easier in the few weeks that I've been back. The world feels unreal and unsteady.

I look up and see the deer heads on the wall. All eight of them seem to want to tell me their stories. They are gone, though, in this world, like they were when they used to haunt my dreams in my first life. I want to reach out and comfort them, but I know they feel no more. I hate that the walls of my family room seem to be a celebration of death because of those deer heads; I feel for them. They're now sad, sacrificial trophies of the way that my dad liked to kill animals for fun.

As a child, I'd look into their vacant, once-vibrant eyes and feel as though I could perfectly relate to them. After all, my dad had tried to kill me, too. He'd threatened my life, perhaps with the same gun that actually killed those deer.

How could anyone stand this? How did I deal with it the first time around? Perhaps because of my ignorance of any other choice. When I look back on it, I see a fearful little girl who was feeling all alone in the world. I remember what it was like to be living in the perpetual state of dread that came from going to bed every night thinking I would never wake up again because Daddy threatened to kill me in my sleep; then again, he also threatened to kill me while I was awake.

I knew that he could completely snap at any time, but nobody dared to show me any sympathy or check in to see how I was feeling. I was just expected to deal with it and get over it all over again every day. That's a lot to expect from any fourth grader, let alone one as completely lacking in confidence as I was.

I always felt that kids were more resilient than adults, and now I know that to be true. I'm not as freshly prepared for anything as I was when I was in this position before. Now I have an awareness of exactly how wrong it all is, and it's making things harder.

I rush from the den to my bedroom. I aim to lose myself in sleep for a little bit. Sleep isn't willing to have anything to do with me tonight, though. I lie awake thinking about how scary it was to try to go to sleep after Dad threatened to turn on the gas from the hot water heater and kill us all. I remember all too well how he said it would be better if we all died. I twist and turn while that renewed fear eats away at me.

My mind wanders, perhaps to protect me from the fact that I am once again living my worst nightmares. I have to do something. I won't be a victim. I won't be a helpless child. Just as I start to nod off, I hear movement in the hall.

My eyes open so wide that I immediately feel afraid that they could be seen even in the pitch black of midnight. I immediately try to stop my breathing from becoming labored with the weight of my fear. All the power in our house has been out since dusk, and I'd escaped to bed without asking for dinner. Now I hope and pray that he'll leave me alone. I feel desperate to disappear.

Suddenly, though, the footsteps that I hear along with the creaking of the wood diminish the hope that I cling to with all my might. My body becomes rigid, and I am ready to go into flight or fight mode. I will not let him hurt me tonight.

"I'm in control; no one can hurt me," I whisper the partial affirmation to myself as I quickly and quietly sit upright in bed.

I lie back down, and I slowly let go of my fears as sleepiness overcomes me. I fall asleep near dawn as my mind is still spinning with the horror and fear of it all.

Chapter 11 ~ Swan Song

I inhale and exhale, taking in the fragrant air. It's the spring of 1989 for the second time in my…life. I guess the word is life. After all, I still have breath, bones, feelings, and awareness. What else can this be?

I knock on the door of Maddie Jenkins, but there is no answer. I haven't seen her or the mysterious little girl in the window since the first Sunday I was back in time. We shared casual conversation and hot chocolate, and I had hoped to be friends with the teen.

Maddie is probably the most mature person I could hope to befriend. Since I'm in the child's body that serves as my current shell, nobody takes me seriously. Beyond that, I can't shake the feeling that there was something different about her.

I wait for 15 minutes before I'm willing to admit that Maddie isn't home. If she is home, she is not going to answer the door for me. Davey is supposed to be babysitting me, so I go home.

I feel resigned as I walk back in my front door. The weight of the world is on my shoulders.

"Hey, Nina," Davey says as he comes to sit on the sofa beside me.

"Hey," I say, looking at him nervously. "You're still staying with me, tonight, right?"

I can smell the alcohol on his breath, but I rest my head on his shoulder anyway. If he still wants to go out, I know that I have to do something drastic. I know that I will do whatever it takes to save him. If he gets a DUI, that might push Dad completely over the edge, and I couldn't bear to lose Mom and Davey again.

"Listen, ya know, maybe you're not so crazy."

"What are you saying? You really will stay home?" I ask.

"You're about my favorite person in the world. This means a lot to you. I said I'd stay home, and I will. So tell me, what's on the tube tonight?"

I hand him the copy of "TV Guide" and rest my head on his shoulder again. I am exhausted. I feel physically tired, but I know it's more that I'm feeling emotionally traumatized. This is all too much for me to handle.

"You know what?" Davey says after thumbing through tonight's programming schedule. "Screw this stuff. Wanna watch a movie?"

"Yeah! Let's!" I exclaim.

Ah, everything is going to be okay.

"I tell ya what," he says, "I'll even let you pick the movie. My one request is that it not include princesses or weddings. Deal?"

"Deal," I eagerly agree.

I rush to my small collection of VHS tapes on the bottom shelf of the entertainment center. It's quick to see that Davey's stipulations have eliminated more than half of the movies I own. I resign myself to a movie I know well: *The Adventures of Baron Munchausen*.

I pull it from Davey's shelf; I figure that picking his favorite movie can provide extra motivation for him to stay with me tonight. As we watch the movie, I notice Robin Williams, and I wonder if he can be saved. It's gotten a bit too easy for me to get lost in daydreams of saving celebrities and the world at large through my bizarre transportation back in time. I still haven't quite wrapped my head around it.

Sometime during the movie, I must have fallen asleep because I wake up to find that the tape has ended. The television's off the air. I forgot how weird it is to see the *Poltergeist*-style static on the screen.

I wipe the sleep out of my eyes when I hear some rattling. I look at the clock beside the television, and I see that it's three o'clock in the morning.

Of course I'm awake. I can never sleep through the night. Since I know that I won't get back to sleep no matter how hard I try, I give up the notion of further rest. I discover what the rattling was; Davey is stumbling through the door, steadying himself by grabbing the wall. He did go out after all. I start to pray that nothing went wrong.

"You okay?" I ask stupidly.

"Am I okay?" he laughs.

He starts to walk towards me ever so slowly. As he approaches, I smell the whiskey sours that he so likes to devour. The scent is so strong that I wonder whether he spilled them on his shirt or bathed in them.

"Gah," I say through sudden tears that sting my eyes, "Davey, you gotta promise me not to drive when you've been drinking. No more."

"Who told you I dr...drove?" he asks half-heartedly as he falls to the sofa so carelessly that it bumps up against the wall and makes a loud noise.

"Keep quiet. If Mom and Dad wake up, they're gonna freak," I scold in whispered tones.

"You...Neenee, you have been acting weird ever since...that birthday party," he says.

"I know. I'm sorry. I love you so much, and I wish that I could explain."

"See. You're talking like you're a damn grown-up. Ah, I'm sorry. I shouldn't talk like that in front of you. I'm gonna be in so much trouble."

"Davey, if I told you something that sounded far out of the scope of anything you're actually able to believe...I mean, if I told you a thing..."

"Say anything," he half-speaks and half-sings rather quietly.

I scoot closer to my brother, and he pulls me up onto his lap. I can't help but let a giggle escape my lips. Even when he's drunk, even as I know how stressful things are for both us, nothing is better than hanging out with my brother.

"There's something I want to say," I explain.

"Well, say it," he jokingly demands.

I sit down, and I try to summon the courage to tell him about my life for the past 27 years. I want to tell him about what adulthood is all about and how tragic it will be if we don't placate Dad somehow. I long to express exactly how much I've missed him and how these moments together are better than anything I ever imagined.

"I'm gonna wait 'til you're sober," I finally say.

"If I can help it, I'll never be sober again," he scoffs.

"I can't wait, can I?" I say, mostly to myself.

"Look, just get it off your chest. I can take it."

"You'll believe me? No matter how crazy it sounds?"

"Of course, I will, Neen."

"Well, you've got to get it together. We can't do anything to provoke Dad. I mean it. I really do. Look, I...I...Do you believe that time travel is possible?"

"Oh, okay. Yeah, right. Like Marty McFly and Peggy Sue, huh? Or like Superman in *Somewhere in Time*? I told Mom not to let you watch so much TV."

"You're not taking me seriously. You promised you would."

"I am. I really am," he lies.

"I'm just messing with you. Forget it. I just am trying to be more grown-up. I am 10 now, ya know?"

"Yeah, you're really getting up there in years."

"Exactly. I'm going back to bed. You gonna be okay down here fending for yourself?"

"Fending for myself? You don't say phrases like that. Holy shit. Were you being real with me? You really think you traveled through time?"

Oh, this is my chance! I want to tell him everything.

"Yeah, I was serious. I don't mean to blame you, though. I know it's sounding like that. And, hey, I don't even know the full reasons. It's just a guess, but I think that Dad can't handle it when you get a DUI."

"What the hell, Nina. How did you know that I got caught to-night?" he asks. "And you know what? Afterwards, on the way home, I drank some more. I just don't care anymore."

"You have to care. How do you think Dad's going to react?"

"That's not my problem. You worry too much."

"He's going to kill himself after he kills you and Mom. He's going to try to kill me, too. I got away last time, but I probably won't this time. I wished I hadn't survived it the first time!"

"How did you manage to get away?" he says in such a condescend-ing way that I know he doesn't believe me at all.

I try to find the words to explain, but then tears fill my eyes. I can't say the words. After all these years, I feel just as guilty. Survivor's guilt is a nasty beast.

"How the hell can you say something that horrible? That is not funny. I know Dad's made some empty threats lately, but he's just your general asshole. He's not a killer. And…"

"Shhh, keep it down. They'll awake up!" I beg.

I start to panic. I see that I've struck a nerve in Davey, which is something I never intended to do. I see his transition from the sweet, sensitive brother I adore to something unnatural and controlled by his worst fears. He is up pacing around, and he starts to throw things around. For a second, he looks far too much like Dad.

"Please! Davey, do you want Dad and Mom to wake up? Do you know how mad they'll be?"

"You know the reason I'm never having children? Because of the way you turned out!" Davey screamed. "And having to babysit you all the time as if I am some damned parent! You're a pest!"

That is exactly what he told me in his first life when I lost him. Those were among his last words to me. The waterworks start. Oh, I hate to sob in front of other people, especially Davey when he's this angry. I berate myself in a million ways. This is what I get for trying to control the situation.

"I certainly understand why you've always been afraid that some-one will murder you," he added. "I wish I could get away with it."

I hear noise upstairs and footsteps. Mom and Dad are awake, and it sounds like they are coming down the stairs. Now I hear the sound of the key in the gun cabinet that rests at the bottom of the stairs.

I think: *Oh no. It's happening all over again.*

I hate myself for once again running out into the night, but I can't stop myself. As my feet hit the pavement, and I race away from my house, I hear the cruel sound of gunshots. I can't stop. I'm hysterical, but my feet don't stop carrying me away from it all. I pick up speed, and I don't know if I'll ever be able to stop.

I run until I arrive at the beach, and I would race into the Gulf if I wasn't so exhausted that I drop to the sand in a breathless desperation, gasping for air and giving up all at once.

Chapter 12 ~ Exploit

It happened all over again. I couldn't stop it. I've berated myself all my life for not being able to save my family, and now it seems that I was brought back in time just to relive the torture all over again.

Because Mom and Dad were both estranged from their families, with no true friends to speak of, it was up to me to identify the bodies. Everything seemed to be up to me, including the responsibility for their deaths. Surely there is something I could have done. How could I fail Mom and Davey twice?

I have no ability to feel a single thing in this moment. I hurt to my limits, then I just stop hurting until the cycle starts all over again. I start to put one foot in front of the other. Something has to give, so I'll just put feelings away for another day.

I walk into the funeral home with some friendly social worker named Jane. She takes my hand, and she looks more uncomfortable than I feel. I remember how nobody knew what to say to me the first time around, and it makes me want to take care of Jane. I don't want her to say the insensitive things I heard when I was first coping with all the losses.

"I don't want to hurt your feelings, but can I go in there alone? I'd like some privacy while I plan the burials," I say.

"You know, you're handling this a little too well," Jane says, but she squeezes my hand and nods her head yes. I'm getting my way.

I sit and listen to the owner of the funeral home as he explains what my options are for burying my mother, my father, and my brother. This one thought keeps repeating itself in my head: *What a heartless loser.*

At first I wasn't sure if I was being fair to the businessman, but my rage boils over as he goes on. So much for casting all feelings aside! Josh Riley, who apparently owns a total of three funeral homes, looks at me with an illusory compassion; he expresses concern about my feelings as though I'm his best friend.

Josh had been hesitant to deal with a child at first. However, after I explained that I was in charge of making the decisions regarding the funeral and burial of three people, he acquiesced rather quickly.

I take a deep breath in and slowly release it. Josh looks down at his desk, pretending to be deep in thought. I have a strong suspicion that he does this for every grieving widow or adult child that walks through his door. He told me that he's been helping the bereaved for a decade, so I imagine that it's a sales ploy that he has perfected during his ten years as a funeral director.

When Josh looks up, a deeper emotion seems to fill his whole being as he continues his speech, "I know that you want to honor your family's memory in the best way that you can, and I have to suggest the top range caskets."

"I already chose the caskets through a catalog. I ordered them," I explain matter-of-factly. "They will be here tomorrow."

"If you buy the casket elsewhere, I'm afraid that all the services that are generally given complimentary with the purchase of a casket will now be charged to you at a higher rate than the general price list. I wish that I could do something about that, but those services are simply a thank you for your patronage. I'd like to help make this time easier."

I know this is just a well-rehearsed speech. Anybody who actually took the time to pay attention to the person sitting before him would realize that it's smart to change up that kind of jargon so that a kid could understand it. I fear for any actual child who would have to deal with him.

"So you'll make this time a little harder if I don't pay 500 percent over retail? That is, quite frankly, unethical. It's a blatant violation of the intent of the federal regulations that state that one can buy a casket from competitors."

"I would never do anything outside the law. I understand that you are grieving..."

"Don't you dare try to placate me!"

My anger was coming out like fire, and I'm sure he'd never had a ten-year-old call him out on his shady tactics. He fidgets and looks at the clock.

"Perhaps you'd like some tea? A soda?" Josh asks.

"How much, tell me, will these services cost? I am holding the general price list that you originally gave my social worker. Now, in writing, I want to know what exactly you are trying to charge me?"

"You know what? I can see you are upset. I can see that you are mad."

"Scheming little creep, you don't know anything about me or my feelings. Like I said, I ordered special coffins already for my mom and my brother. For my dad, I would like the cheapest, ugliest wooden coffin you have to offer. If it is a cent above the retail comparison figures that I have amassed here, I will go forward with my legal complaints against this establishment."

"I understand that the economy..." continues Josh, refusing to give up on any sale.

"The economy isn't destroying me, but my father almost did. I have no desire to honor him with some rose-colored metal he won't even know surrounds him for eternity. When I come back tomorrow, please be prepared for my payment for exactly how much it is worth with only the fair mark-up that all the other local establishments would want. Don't think I won't triple check that."

"Wait, Nina," Josh is begging now. "Kid…"

"Yes?" I sigh.

"It's a deal, okay? My manager is going to be really mad at me, but I don't want anyone walking out of this office without at least the slight solace of knowing that plans are finalized. I will have it, and here..."

He writes down the price.

"So, if someone's too sad to do research or too inexperienced to know how to protect themselves, you basically take huge chunks of money from people when they're at their most vulnerable?" I ask him. "Are you really too cold-hearted to give a damn about that?"

I run out of the funeral home. I sit on the sidewalk. I just plop down. Tears flow from my eyes, and I cannot take it anymore. It's all too much. I cannot handle this.

I want to go back. I'd give anything to go back to my old life. I want to go back to being the fat 37-year-old. I wouldn't commit suicide. I wouldn't even think about it anymore. I had no reason to feel responsible for things then. I want my old life. I don't care. I just want to go back to my old world and my old life. I cannot live through this again. The grief overwhelms me.

Chapter 13 ~ Visiting Day

What I love and loathe the most about gravestones are their mysteries. I mean, they leave out all the important and interesting things about a person. The overly generalized nature of something so lasting strikes me as absurd. In the end, the exact date of birth or death really doesn't matter in comparison to all the days that were fully lived.

Also, gravestones merely note the roles we fulfilled. Our existence in relation to one another as daughter, wife, mother, or granddaughter is important when we're alive, but these roles are just parts we all play in the end. I want to know what makes someone special.

When I see the gravestones of strangers, I want to know what those people most wanted for themselves. I long to know the best and worst moments of their lives, which works of art spoke to them, and how they loved other people. I want to know their stories, and I want those stories to be told from their perspectives. Instead, gravestones just tell cold, hard facts in the most impersonal way possible.

Davey was someone else entirely from what his tombstone declared. The facts on his headstone are simple. David Gregory Newman was born on December 1, 1969 and died on April 16, 1989. The marker declares that he was a beloved brother and son.

As if to add insult to the most bare and misleading details of Davey's life, I fear that the ugly, polished slab of granite will now forever reign over Davey's buried body and speak for him. It mercilessly leaves out the most interesting and loving aspects of who he was. After all, nobody ever called him David Gregory Newman; he was Davey to anyone who spent a minute in his company.

Even the color of his tombstone seems to mock how full of life he was. He was all the colors of the rainbow, and he always hated grey. He wouldn't even choose Sergeant Gray when we played our "Clue" VCR game. He thought the name was too boring, and he wanted to play an exciting character. He wanted to be loved, and he most certainly was.

The only thing I can do is try to bring a little bit of him to this horrific display of lies. I place forget-me-nots in front of his grave.

Chapter 14 ~ Thirsty

I think: *Don't look for me here. I don't want to be known.*

I dislike the foster family that takes me in. I don't even spend an hour there before I make an excuse to leave. I rush to my old neighborhood, but I still can't find Maddie. I keep rushing away, my forward momentum more to do with everything I'm fleeing than a desire to go towards anything in particular.

I soon realize where I need to go. I rush into the blood donor center. I have to start doing something good for other people again, or I am not going to survive the second loss of my family. Somehow I must get back in the swing of things. If I am going to go on, I need to start with something small and find my way to doing big, bold things.

Giving blood is something I tried to do every two months in my original life. I liked the feeling of helping others in some small, anonymous way. It kept me going, too, during times when suicide became a more tempting option.

"I'm here to give blood," I tell the receptionist.

"Well, that's wonderful! Bless your heart," she says to me kindly. "I tell you what, I wish more people in the world were like you. What's your name, sweetheart?"

"I'm Nina," I reply. "Nina Newman."

"Nice to meet you, Nina. My name is Lisa. Now, tell me something. Did your mom or dad bring you?"

"No, I'm here by myself."

"Ah, I see. Well, you know, honey, we have an age limit on who can give blood. If you have your parents' consent, you have to be at least sixteen. If you're by yourself, you'd have to be at least seventeen. Unless you are really youthful for your age, I'm afraid you can't donate yet. However, when you get a little bit older, we would be so very thankful to see you."

"I have to give blood. I always do," I say, then gulp as I feel my eyes bulge.

"You do, huh?" Lisa replies.

I can tell that Lisa is amused by my claim. I was initially scared that I'd given away a secret, but she isn't going to take me seriously. This is the first time that I've slipped up, and I managed to do it in front of a nurse and the receptionist. Maybe they'll put me away now. I swallow and look down, trying to think of what to say. The woman at the front desk smiles at me.

"I tell you what. I bet the rules have changed since the last time you gave blood," she continues. "You are such a sweetheart. Did you see that television documentary on how we all have a responsibility to give blood?"

I nod my head yes. It's a lie. It's just something I've done for years. Every two months, I give blood; it saves lives. How is that so complicated?

"Like I said, I wish we could accept it, but it's not okay just yet. But, wow, am I impressed with you. Here, have a few stickers. We only give these out to the real heroes, you know?"

Lisa hands me the stickers, and I force myself to smile and utter a quick "thank you" before letting the frown return to my face.

"Oh, don't look so glum," she continues. "Keep yourself healthy and strong, and then you'll be able to help us out so much when you get a little bit older. I tell you what, though. Would you like to help out in another way?"

I nod my head yes. I need to do something. If I just stay still, I'm going to burst.

"See that bulletin board over there?" Lisa asks.

I nod my head yes as I look in the direction where she points. It is huge. There is no way I could miss it.

"I see it," I reply with a smile.

"Okay, well then. You need to go over there and check out all the opportunities we have for sweet people just like you. That's a volunteer board. Organizations from all over post to it when they need a helping hand. Some of them accept kids as volunteers."

"Oh, that's great."

"Take one of those chairs in the lobby over to the board and take your time exploring it. Feel free to use my phone here to call any of them that interests you, so just come back here when you're done."

"Thank you, Lisa."

I walk over to the board, and I'm instantly overwhelmed. I get the idea that I'm supposed to choose charity work by what I would most enjoy, but I don't know if that's such a good idea.

What I want to ultimately do is spend my time giving back as effectively as possible. If the only thing that motivates someone to do volunteer work is having fun or socializing at the same time, that's one thing, and there's nothing wrong with that. What I want to do, though, is make as much of a difference as I can.

I also consider nurturing my creativity. Nothing has helped me more in this life than the *Autumn Joy* painting I discovered so long ago. Maybe making my own kind of art could help someone somewhere.

I continue to peruse the board. An ad for volunteers at the local animal shelter catches my attention. It's quite difficult to articulate my connection and deep affinity for animals in a way that is easily understood. I used to hesitate when I was inclined to donate blood, because I had witnessed so much of the cruelty that human beings are capable of inflicting on animals and other people. I wondered if, by saving someone, it wouldn't contribute to ultimately more harm. Now I know that saving anyone who needs it is a moral imperative.

Now I start to consider the possibilities. I decide that I need to live for helping others and to somehow figure out what is going on with me. I'm convinced that there must be a reason for it all.

Chapter 15 ~ Sweet 16

I had to face the truth. I can't really let my guard down or be my true self with anyone, and I won't be able to for the rest of my life. Carrying the secret of going back through time is nearly as disorienting as actually doing it.

I turned sixteen for the second time a few months ago, but I am still counting the years I had in my other life, the one that refuses to feel like a distant memory or a daydream. I consider my real age to be 43. The mirror says that I am really 16, though, and I won't argue with that. I am almost through masquerading as a child. It's a good thing, too, because I feel as though I am about to explode.

I tried to figure out what's going for so long and in so many ways that it just became part of my renewed nature. I walk down the street and see a face that looks familiar. Sometimes I run into people I know but haven't met in this timeline, and I still occasionally say things that people haven't yet told me. That freaks them out every time.

I waited on pins and needles for the release of "Gaia" on its release date. I missed this Olivia Newton-John album more than any other music from my first life. I love the way that the music sounds from the first note of "Trust Yourself" through the lovely ending of "The Way of Love." Now that I have the album, I plan to listen to it as I drive to and from school each day.

Although I was homeschooled within my foster family in the wake of the tragedy, that's now a thing of the past because I have to leave my foster family. Things got too awkward there. Things always get awkward because I just can't let my guard down for even a second with this secret I carry.

So back to my old school it is. I take dance seriously and regularly win competitions. I've also become an effective altruist, but there's still so much that I need to learn if I'm going to help others in the best ways possible.

As I go into the classroom on my first day back at school, I realize how badly I want to make friends. I look around for a kid who seems the most in need of a friend. That's when I spot Penny.

Penny is sitting all by herself at the back of the Algebra classroom. I remember that it took us two years to actually speak to each other when I was first in high school, and, although I wanted to be friends with her, never tried to be. That's just silly, and my once crippling shyness was exorcized long ago.

"I'm Nina. What's your name?"

"Penny. Where are you from?"

"What does it matter?" I ask, hoping I didn't come off as harsh; I just cannot bear to answer anything that could lead to questions about my family.

"You ashamed of where you come from?"

"Something like that."

"You're ashamed of me?"

"No. Geez, why would I be?"

"At my other school, no kids wanted to be seen with me."

"I don't give a shit about what anyone thinks of me. If I did care, I'd want to be seen with you because anybody should be impressed with you. If they're not, they're not worth your thoughts."

What I've just said makes her eyes light up, and she looks at me in a way that she never did before.

"I think we're going to be great friends, Nina. You're not like the other kids around here."

If only she knew how true that was. I could never argue that point anyway. I was eternally a misfit, and somehow that bothers me less and less as time marches on.

Chapter 16 ~ Friends

I dance around the room I share with a foster sister named Allison. She's lovely, but she's not here. I've seen her exactly twice in the few weeks since I arrived. She hangs around the house less than I do. Most foster parents are actually great people who get a terrible and unfair reputation because of the repugnant behaviors of a few bad ones. My new foster family is fine, but I cannot risk getting too attached.

I watch my reflection in the mirrored closet door as I perform grand jetés. I am determined to become the best dancer I can be, and I take any spare moment to practice even the things I mastered years ago. I look my body over and still cannot get used to how much smaller I am. Maybe I'll always feel as though I am an imposter in my own body.

I struggled with my weight constantly in my old lifetime, but somehow it isn't a problem this time around. I have better coping skills and no longer eat my feelings, but I know that weight is more complicated than all that. I'll take it, though. At least one of the more superficial parts of my history isn't repeating itself.

I'm thrilled when my cell phone rings. I know who it will be. Penny, who refuses to let anyone call her by Penelope, is on the line. I'm amazed by how much I care for my friend. I remember Penny being kind to me before, but we have a real friendship now.

"Hey, babe. Did you finish packing last night?" she asks.

"Yeah," I lie. "I'll come over to your place around 6?"

"You bet. Don't forget a change of clothes."

I speak to Penny easily, and we spend most afternoons at her place. Her dad always teases me, and I still envy girls who grow up with dads who tease them and want to protect them.

When Penny and I go out, though, I feel that people are always looking at me funny. She's tall, and I'm short. While I'm naturally curvy even at a low body weight, she's so thin no matter how much she eats. Her southern accent is strong, while mine doesn't come to the surface all that often.

What we have in common is a love for each other. Finding a kindred spirit in this time and place was the last thing I expected. I envy Penny's blissful lack of awareness because it's something that only the very young carry, but we seem to share all the other cravings and passions for life.

Penny and I rush into things head first, so eager to experience every sort of thing we possibly can. We want it all as quickly as we can grasp it, no matter how much pain comes with the pleasures we seek. We don't waste a moment hesitating or second-guessing ourselves.

We are so preoccupied with our lives and friendship that we don't notice prying eyes. We see no signs that we may be in danger, and I don't even consider the possibility that simply knowing me could put someone in harm's way.

Chapter 17 ~ Loves

I arrive at six o'clock on the dot, and Mary, Penny's mother, greets me with a warm hug. She holds on longer than most people do, then wraps a comforting arm around me as she escorts me into the home.

"You are the only person I know who's more punctual than I am," she says.

I think that Mary is horrified by my tough past, and she always goes the extra mile to make me feel appreciated and wanted. It's incredibly wonderful to be in her company. You always feel like the most special person in the world, yet you know that she's also making everyone else in the room feel the exact same way, so you don't have to worry about making them jealous or uncomfortable. It's all in the little things she does, too; she makes no over-the-top gestures.

Mary walks me to Penny's room, and she knocks on the door. I marvel at how respectful she is of her daughter's privacy. Most parents I know would simply shout for their kids from the bottom of the stairs.

"Nina's here," Mary says and winks at me. "Sweetheart, did you ask her to stay for dinner already?"

"You bet," Penny says as she flings open the door to her bedroom. "Thanks, Mom. We can order pizza, right?"

"As you wish," Mary says jovially with a little bow.

It's some kind of joke between them from a movie, but I forget which one. I haven't seen it. Penny quickly pulls me into her room and shuts the door behind us, making me feel a bit sorry for Mary. I wonder what Penny's mom does for fun while we hide out in this bedroom for hours on end.

When I look at Penny again in the bright light of her bedroom, I see that she's been crying. My immediate response is to run to her and try to figure out what is going on, but I second guess myself.

"We should work on homework," Penny says, quickly looking down and avoiding eye contact.

"Yeah, that French quiz is tomorrow."

I sprawl out on the floor, while Penny grabs her French book and creates a study area on her bed. As soon as I've opened my French book to the review page and take out a notebook, I look up. I notice that Penny is trying to stop herself from being emotional, but a tear breaks free and flows down her face.

"I was watching the biography channel earlier. During a tour with Fleetwood Mac, did you know one of the band members left to join a cult? Isn't that stupid?"

"I don't know," I reply, "I guess none of us has it all figured out. Who's to say that what we do is any better than what that guy did?"

"Um, common sense says so," Penny replies, and I hear annoyance just flowing out of her tones.

"I just don't think you're being very fair," I say with a smile as I lay back on the floor.

"So, change of subject. What made you want to be a professional dancer?" Penny asks.

"Well, I'd say the moment I saw a painting," I reply.

"A painting. Like Degas?" Penny smiles.

"No, not even. The painting wasn't of dancers…It was…"

Before I can finish explaining how deeply I was inspired by Leonard's work of art, she has changed the subject yet again. Keeping up with her train of thought is good for me because I'm not thinking of all the worries on my mind. I have to be really present to be able to be her friend, and that is becoming my sanity.

"Penny," I finally say when she has exhausted three other random subjects, "What's going on? I can see that you're upset, and I want to be there for you. Really."

"I asked Keith out," she says as a fresh supply of tears flood her eyes. "And he turned me down, of course."

"He's clueless," I say, but I know the words probably sound hollow in comparison to the enormous pain that rejection brings. "Man, will he ever regret that in time."

"Take me some place pretty," Penny begs.

I do the only thing I know how to do when it comes to my sweet friend; I oblige. We let Mary know that we decided to get dinner out, and off we go.

I put in a mix tape that I made for Penny. I keep it in my car to ensure that she always has music that she loves on hand when we're on the road. She's a big fan of Fleetwood Mac, so I smile when she starts to sing along to "Don't Stop" despite the conversation we had earlier about the cult. We often joke that we should have been teens of the 1970's.

I drive my little car carefully through the tunnel. It looks like Penny may be feeling at least a little bit better, so I dare to try to bring up another topic of conversation.

"Can you believe this tunnel is still named after a man who supported segregation?" I ask.

"That's really messed up," she replies.

That's all she says, though. We usually have passionate discussions about the injustices of the world, and she and I try to figure out what small things we can do to help. By her silence, I can tell my poor friend is devastated. Penny stares out the window with a lifeless expression, even when I stop at a little fast food restaurant and order us both veggie burgers, fries, and Cokes. Before I can even think about anything else, I find myself driving us up to the little Fairhope Pier.

As I start to turn off the car, I notice a gorgeous brown dog with copper around her eyes. She runs alongside a little girl who calls out, "Marta!" When the child reaches down for a hug, her canine companion kisses her right on the nose. I am enchanted by the perfect little dog when Penny's voice reminds me of the problem at hand.

"He called me peerless," Penny fumes as soon as I park the car.

She takes a bite out of her veggie burger, and it doesn't seem to perk up her mood. The same is true for a handful of fries that she stuffs in her mouth. I have already finished off half my meal. Tonight I'm forgetting that I worry way too much about calories, and I'm just going to enjoy myself.

"You know that's a compliment, right? He's probably trying to say that you're one-of-a-kind," I reply, trying to reassure her, but suddenly I see ire in her eyes.

"Of course I know that. Do you think I'm an idiot?"

"No, I'm sorry. I'm just saying. He was trying...I don't know...to tell you how much he likes you, and maybe he turned you down for other reasons...."

"You don't have a clue about men. That's okay. Neither do I," moans Penny.

"You know what? It's probably better that way. Who cares, right? Fries before guys."

With that, I put a fry in my mouth, and she just rolls her eyes at me.

"Not funny, and you're making me hungry all over again," she scolds, but the edges of her lips turn up into a small smile.

"I'm just saying. Keep your priorities in order."

"Like chips before relationships?"

"That's the spirit."

"We're such dorks," she says, "Thank you. I feel just a bit better."

She and I sit in silence for a few minutes, and we watch people enjoying the beach. They say that, if you want to hear a lot of tragic stories, ask a comedian about her childhood. I always wonder about the story of each individual I meet. Everybody has a story that's so very worth telling.

The people on the beach are fascinating to me. A family with five kids takes care to feed all the swans that they see. A teenage boy tries to swim in the water. A couple can't stop kissing as they relax on a beach blanket. I wonder if they have worries on their minds that prevent them from living in the moment, and I wish that they could all find peace and happiness.

Chapter 18 ~ Dance, Nina, Dance

As I perform in what I've determined will be my final dance recital, it's comforting to know that Penny is in the audience. It doesn't even hurt to see all the families surround the other girls after they perform. I am at peace with what's going on with me.

I decided to give up competitive dancing because it occurred to me that my years of experience with dance in my first life gave me an unfair advantage, making the awards meaningless. If you think too hard, you can really take the joy out of a whole lot of things, but that doesn't mean you should avoid the truth.

Really, the past shapes us and sneaks up on us and comes over for tea. It's not really, truly here any longer, though, and we have to let it go at the end of the day. No matter what happened to you, you have the chance to turn it all around on this day within this very minute.

As I dance, I feel really hopeful; it has been a long time since I've thought of ending my life. Maybe that's because, more than ever, I realize how little I know. In comparison to the entire world, I know so little. There are endless possibilities for joy and wonder in the world, and perhaps there is a way to save lives or make people happy that I am not yet even aware of existing. It would be foolish to give up on a world with so much beauty and undiscovered loveliness just because I also see a lot of its horror.

As I step off the stage after my last performance of the night, Penny is there with green roses and open arms. I hug her. We're both seventeen now, and she's had a hard time lately because her parents are divorcing.

"Wow, these are beautiful. Thank you so much for coming. It means the world," I say.

"Let's get out of here," she says, eying all the families gathering around the dancers.

"Can we grab a bite to eat?"

I see that this is not what Penny had in mind. She sighs, perhaps thinking about her diet. We've both put on a couple of pounds lately, but it's not worrying me. I wonder if Penny is considering whether our friendship is worth a delay in her diet. I can tell that she's really annoyed, and it takes everything within me not to simply acquiesce and tell her to forget about it. I really need some kind of release.

Once again, we are sure to indulge in food that's about as devious as we dare to be. We'll probably order veggie burgers at a small diner on the edge of town.

As soon as we are at the diner, I excuse myself and go to the bathroom. I catch a glimpse of myself in the mirror. I can't help but wondering how I would look at 44. I find myself oddly wishing to see my authentic age. I know women pay their fortunes away to look seventeen again, yet I find it so hard to luxuriate in the novelty for long. That's the thing, though. It's not a novelty to me. Is it because it's commonplace and an everyday thing that I'm so quick to wish it away?

As soon as I sit back down at our table, a tired-looking waitress in a depressing, bright yellow uniform approaches our table.

"Hey girls, what will you be having tonight?"

"What do you have that's vegan?" I ask.

"Huh? Say what?" the waitress with weary eyes asks.

Penny gives me the evil eye. I've embarrassed her. Oops. She's cool with vegetarianism, but I forget how much my veganism irritates her. I also forget how rare it is for people to be vegan in the 1990's.

"Um, a veggie burger?" I dare to ask, hoping that they even serve one.

"Ah, I can do that. What about you, sweetie?"

"Well," Penny barks as she takes in the menu with a sweeping glance, "An omelet. Pancakes. Toast, hold the butter, and grape jam. Oh, and a vanilla cappuccino. "

The waitress nods an okay as she takes our menus and rushes off.

"I don't even know why I bother to take a menu. Diners always have that shit," Penny continues, "And, you. Really? A veggie burger for breakfast?"

"The heart wants what it wants," I smile. "Okay, so verdict. What did you think of my dancing? For real?"

"It was perfect. So beautiful."

Penny grins, and her pride in my dancing makes me feel happy. Whatever this friendship means, I'm thankful for it.

She and I are mischievous and fearless together. We share a mutual understanding that life's inevitable tragedies will catch up with us again, so we grab joy as fast as we can wherever we find it. If she forgets, I do a little something to remind her to stay present, breathe in, and take some pleasure from what this single day has to offer.

"What do you want for your future?" she asks me as we wait for our food.

I feel a surge of the guilt that always threatens to blanket every day. Why do I even have a future when Mom and Davey don't?

"I want to create something meaningful. I'm going to learn a new art form now that I'm giving up dance. I want to continue to get better at effective altruism."

"Me, too, on that last thing. Plus," adds Penny. "I want to get married."

"That's the sort of thing that you can't plan for, though," I say, then immediately regret it.

"Yeah, you can. Don't you want to get married?"

Flashes of being pushed against the wall and smothered nearly to death on my wedding night flash through my eyes. Memories of a short-lived, abusive marriage don't go easy on me. It's hard for me to be objective.

"I don't know," I say honestly.

"I do know. I must. It's going to be great. When I get married, he and I better stay together forever," Penny scoffs.

"Yeah, but, I mean, that's what everyone wants. It's not your mom's fault that your dad left."

"Oh, isn't it? She didn't keep him happy. I'd keep my man happy."

"That's not really fair. I've seen your mom with your dad; she treats him like a king," I dare to say.

"Oh, you've seen them together? Do you really think you've seen them together like I have? Besides, yeah, okay. You're right. She does treat him like a king. The thing is, I feel really bad for her. I'd rather a man die than watch him go off and be with another woman, ya know? Oh, that must suck so bad."

"If you'd rather a man die than be happy away from you, that's not love. It's like an obsession or a…possession. But not love."

"Screw you. Besides, I don't even know the guy I'm going to marry yet. I'm just saying."

"Sorry," I laugh.

Sometimes I irritate myself. Sometimes I lose sight of the fact that she really is only seventeen. I should give her a break. My ideals on love get me every time.

Chapter 19 ~ Trip

I am a high school graduate! The ceremony is even more insufferable the second time around, even though this time I bothered to apply myself just slightly more and sit on the stage at the graduation.

For better or worse, Penny and I have remained friends throughout our high school career. She takes me under her wing and helps me find ways to be bold and brave. I keep her somewhat amused, although I don't think I fall so high on the sense of humor spectrum myself.

All I want for my eighteenth birthday is to attend a conference where Leonard Daley is going to do a presentation about art and inspiration. I longed to meet my favorite artist all my life, and I feel an aching need to actually see him in person. Penny one-ups that desire and gets us both tickets to Paris for the conference. I wasn't expecting anything of the sort, and the surprise overwhelms me.

Penny has a way of getting me the best birthday presents, and her family encourages her. Even though they're divorced, both her parents keep in close contact with me. I still wonder if they just feel sorry for me, but I dare to hope that I'm truly loved. I don't feel lovable, and it's weird to think that they may love me.

As Penny and I walk on a path near the Eiffel Tower, the beauty of the place strikes me as being far more intense than any movie or book could ever reveal. It's hard to focus on something that lovely for very long without your mind wandering, though. It kind of feels like taking it all in would ruin you for ordinary life.

Penny suggests we go to a bar. I don't want to waste my time in Paris at a mere bar, but I can't bring myself to refuse the request. She has been so generous and kind with this elaborate gift. I follow her as she searches for just the right bar.

As we stroll, I start to think about how foolish I had been to pay so little attention to world events. I'd felt powerless to make a difference, so I just ignored the horrors of the world. Had I been interested in sports, perhaps I could have found a way to buy a winning team. If I'd at least read the finance section, maybe I could make wise investments. I knew the basic, major successes, but I never really paid attention to when certain things hit it big. How had I managed to get through life while ignoring so much?

I wonder about all the decisions that we make. I marvel at the impact they could potentially have on others and how they feed off one another. Tonight, if we keep the bartender late, maybe his wife won't be awake when he gets there. Maybe this was the night they were going to conceive a child, yet now they won't. Maybe the person who could solve the complexities of war in the world won't be born because of one thing I accidentally do differently this time around. I know that's absurd, but I find any possibility racing through my mind.

Paris is just so beautiful that I don't want to touch anything here. I'm afraid that I will somehow taint it. I never got to this magical city in my first awareness of life.

"Let go here," Penny suggests.

I laugh when I look at the place she's chosen. The bar has a United States theme, with the flag on display alongside memorabilia from classic American television shows. I adore my country, and I have no qualms about gobbling down American food and drinks. It's just that the bar seems out of place and odd. Sometimes we look for signs of home despite the fact that we've gone to great lengths to get away from it all for a bit.

I tend to dislike any bars because none of them give me the contact high that watching an episode of *Cheers* does. Nobody really knows my name, and the bars I've tried all tend to smell rather leathery, somewhat stale, or oddly cathedral-like.

I refrain from complaining, though, and try to savor the moment for what it is. Penny goes to the bathroom as soon as we settle into a booth at the bar, leaving me to sit by myself. I see it as an excuse to read and reach for the book in my bag. I've never been comfortable in bars and dislike dealing with drunken strangers, so I am not too excited when I see a man approaching the table.

"Hello," the man says, "You here with anybody?"

"Yes," I say with as kind a smile as I can manage.

I never want to hurt anybody's feelings, but I lived without attention from men for so long that I don't know how to deal with it now. At least for me, going through life as an overweight woman was like being invisible to most men and an outlet for the anger of others. Now, all these years later, my spirit still feels like I'm that same woman who received so much rejection.

"Why has he left you alone for so long?" he asks.

"How would you know how long I've been here?" I reply with a far angrier tone than I'd intended.

"Just a guess."

I realize that the man looks familiar. However, he speaks with an English accent, and I can't remember meeting any man from England in recent years.

"I'm on the rebound, so I just kind of need some alone time," I lie.

"Yeah," he sighs and frowns in a way that makes me almost pity him. Almost.

"This is just kind of a private weekend for me. I'm sorry. I just kind of need to do my thing here."

"Yeah. Look, sorry I was so persistent. I hope I didn't scare you."

"No harm, no foul."

He smiles, then awkwardly retreats. I get back to my Alice Hoffman book, and it helps me daydream about magic and love as if both were real in my life today.

Luckily, Penny returns and gets her fix of the place almost immediately. She and I decide to call it a night. Our first night in Paris should be spent mostly sleeping, I conclude.

When I go back to my hotel room, I stop in front of its majestic mirror. The full-length mirror shows me from head to toe. I evaluate myself as objectively as possible. All I see are features that could be prettier. I used to feel sorry for people who got a lot of plastic surgery, but I learned to not judge most situations or choices as I experienced more things in life.

I shake it off. I have more important things to consider than how I look. I realize that I'm only getting preoccupied with the way I look because I may be able to meet the great Mr. Daley tomorrow. When I think of what his art has meant to me, I feel all kinds of happy inside.

Chapter 20 ~ If Wishes Were Artists

You probably don't want to take advice from me. I'm just a woman trying to understand the wondrous world. However, I do feel qualified to say that, if you're not in the habit of going to beaches or mountains, stand on both as often as possible, because they will challenge you to leave any notions that you are all-powerful out of your head. They're sure to help you feel a sense of freedom that comes from appreciating the world for what it actually is.

I feel like I am in the midst of some epic force of nature as Penny and I walk into the conference area of the hotel. I clutch her hand when I suddenly get terrified. I don't want to appear ungrateful, but I want to cut and run. It's too much pressure.

"Penny, will you hate me if I tell you that I'm ready to leave?" I say quietly.

"Yes," she says, then a big grin takes over her face. "Of course not, but I will be disappointed in you. Come on, this is going to be fun. What's the worst that can happen?"

"I can totally make a complete idiot out of myself," I say, "You know, I think this was a bad idea. It's better to leave fantasies in their place. I can't deal with this. What if he's a real asshole? In a way, that would ruin the painting for me. I couldn't enjoy it any more. If I can't enjoy that art any more, do you know what...."

"Just shut up," she says, then she gives me a big hug.

"I'm sorry," I say sincerely.

"Hand me that interview and pic of him you brought with us, will ya?" she asks.

I reach in the bag and find it quickly, handing it over to her. She studies the photo and hands it back to me. I look at her, wondering what she's doing.

"It's okay. Now, don't freak or anything, but I see him over there. He must be getting ready for his panel discussion, and a group of people are already gathering around to talk to him. Now's your chance. It looks like a family is about to move along. They're shaking his hand."

I take a deep breath.

"I mean it, Penny. I just can't."

"There he is. Go say something," she insists.

She's not going to put up with my insecurities. We've come too far for the conference. I turn in the direction she's facing, and I notice Leonard from across the room. He looks nearly identical to his photograph, and someone makes him smile. When they do, it's almost as though the photo I cherished of him from the magazine has been recreated. He's a man whose eyes sparkle; few men have sparkling eyes that are so lit up my some kind of spiritual wholeness or at least a deep joy from within. I wonder if he's truly that happy, or if he's merely trying to make others feel such merriment.

Before I can make sense of anything else, Penny is pulling me towards him. Because I don't want to look like a foolish schoolgirl, I pick up the pace so it looks like we are merely walking side by side. I realize that we must look like we are charging towards him, and I start laughing. That stops Penny in her tracks, and she puts her hands on her hips as she looks at me.

"Now what?" she asks as exasperation seems to flow from her pores.

"You are just the best friend ever. Thank you for this," I say.

"Don't thank me. Just get over there."

When I hesitate, Penny starts pulling me again, so I pick up the pace. Once again, we are charging towards him, but I stifle my laughter. The terror within builds. We are now within two feet of the man I've admired for so long, and I find myself staring at him. Before I realize what's happening, he is regarding us with a warm smile.

"Hello there," he says. "Thanks for coming here today. I'm Leonard Daley."

"Hi. I know. I'm Penny. This is my friend Nina. We came all the way from the States to see you."

"Wow, really? What an honor. Thank you," he says sincerely. "I hope you enjoy the presentation."

"*Autumn Joy*. Wow, it's such an inspiration," I manage to say, then I want to kick myself. I have never been so incapable of speaking in an articulate way.

"Wow, ya know...."

Leonard start to say something to us, but he's interrupted by an angry-looking woman in a form-fitting business suit. I feel instant outrage. Now I'll never know what words were going to come out of his mouth. It feels like something valuable has been shamelessly stolen.

"Mr. Daley, it's time to get started," the woman says, then gives me and Penny a side-eye stare.

"Sorry, we didn't mean to interrupt," I say to her.

"Don't be silly. I was thrilled to meet you. Stay after the presentation, and we can all chat a bit," Leonard says sweetly as he steps between us and the irritated handler.

Penny and I look at each other, and it's all I can do to keep from squealing. I cannot find words to form a response, so I hope she understands that my gaze is a desperate call for help.

"That would be great," Penny says, "We'll see you then."

I'm thankful that she is able to still speak like a regular person because I cannot. Leonard shakes my hand, then he shakes Penny's hand.

He makes us feel heard and appreciated before stepping away with the seemingly angry woman.

Chapter 21 ~ Through the Eyes of Love

Leonard strikes me as someone who's so completely wonderful. I've met a few of my heroes. It's one of the things I've been exploring and doing for myself since I've been given so much time to rethink and relive my life. However, I never felt an all-encompassing feeling of affection for someone like I felt for him from the moment we first met

I know it's more than appreciation for Leonard's art, which I have in spades. I can't deny that his art makes me feel exceedingly ecstatic. There is a lot more to this man, though. He's even far more incredible than his art. I find myself wondering how he sees the world and resist the temptation to fill in the blanks with my own expectations.

The presentation was heavenly, and he chatted with us for an hour after it was over. Penny had the nerve to invite him to hang out with us at the America-themed bar she discovered last night. I wanted to squeal with delight because he agreed, then it made me want to scream at her because, of all the beautiful places we could go with Leonard Daley in the city, a dark bar seems to be such a poor choice. I have hope for this experience with Leonard, though.

I am awed that he actually wants to spend time with me of his own volition. That's a shock. I never feel deserving of anyone's time, yet here is the most amazing man that I've ever met spending time with me. Life is weird.

I find myself once again clutching Penny's hand as we walk in the bar. We're early, but he is here already. I spot him across the room, and

I am the one dragging Penny along this time. I have to refrain from running into his arms.

As we approach, Leonard stands and waves. He moves aside so that we can move into the booth.

"Nice choice," I say, referring to the booth, but I'm not even sure if I managed to make that simple thought clear. I can't bring myself to say another word. I just gape like an idiot.

"Well, thank you. Thank you very much," he says. "So, tell me. What do you think of Paris?"

I am about to respond when we are interrupted. I want to throw a tantrum like a toddler because I need at least five minutes at a time to converse with him. I may never get another chance to see this man again.

A woman shouts into a microphone as though she has no idea how a microphone works. She announces that it's time for karaoke, and that she demands someone come up and perform. She threatens to sing if there are no volunteers. As a preview, she sings a few notes, and hearing them can only be described politely as a special kind of torture. I look towards Penny, hoping she'll suggest someplace else where the three of us can go.

"Come on. Don't you want to give it a try?" Leonard asks me.

I smile, but I'm feeling too shy to respond. Realizing that nobody else in the bar is going to take the woman up on her offer, Leonard goes up and volunteers. He's certainly a good sport, and I'm going to get to see him sing. How perfect!

Leonard commands the stage like a rock star when he walks out to do karaoke. I marvel at the man's confidence. He is not quite as secure as he has every right to be, but he charms the crowd with what seems like an innate grace. If I was him, I imagine how full of myself I'd be. I find myself wishing that he would truly perceive his own greatness.

I try to imagine which song he's chosen to sing. I think maybe a new song because he seems so cultured yet cool. He probably knows all the latest songs, while I prefer to listen to music from decades ago with a few exceptions. I wish we were a bit further into the future, though, because I really miss Taylor Swift's *1989*. I hope that doesn't get altered with this new timeline somehow.

Suddenly I hear the first two notes, and I know exactly which song he's chosen. It's "Faith" by George Michael, and I smile at the fun choice. It's definitely a song that's been getting radio play for around a decade in this timeline. He is putting his heart and soul into it as though it is a serious performance on a world stage, and his voice is bold and strong.

I know "Faith" well enough to sing along, but I wisely don't. I enjoy the moment, and it's during the performance that I find myself falling deeply in love with him. He looks embarrassed, and I want to tell him that he's the closest thing to perfect I could ever see.

Chapter 22 ~ Going Home

The three-day dream excursion to Paris flies by way too quickly, and Penny and I both vow that we will plan a month-long girls' getaway to the city as soon as we possibly can. One can never get enough of Paris.

I offer Penny the window seat on the flight home, and she gratefully accepts. I sit down beside her, and I am still giddy from the times we spent in the city with Leonard. He hung out with us once per day for the entire three days we were there. I never dreamed he'd be so nice and friendly.

"Nobody should love that hard," Penny says when she takes one look at my face and sees the look in my eyes. "Especially with a man you just met."

"This was the most special week of my life," I tell Penny. "Thank you."

"You're welcome," she says with a smile.

"Oh, my goodness," I tell her. "See that guy over there? I met him at the bar the first night of our trip."

I cannot believe my eyes. There is the stranger who came on to me at the bar. When I see him on the plane, I instantly flash on where I've seen him before. It was in front of the Show Biz Pizza Place when I first woke up back in time. He was a teenager in an oversized suit, but now he wears black jeans and a black button-down shirt.

"Well, that bar's a mecca for tourists. Tourists fly home. Don't freak. You don't think he's flying back home to stalk us, do you? Get a grip," Penny says with a laugh.

She's a bit harsher than usual, but it does make me see the absurdity of my freak out. And I cannot tell her why it really upsets me; I can't tell her that I saw him once in front of a pizza parlor. She'd really think I was nuts and hallucinating.

Chapter 23 ~ Summer in the City

Penny and I decide to go to Manhattan for the summer after our exciting trip to Paris. We daydreamed about it all during high school, but we are really going for it now.

I'm thinking a lot about the creepy man on the plane, and I get more paranoid. The more focused I am on what makes me so different than the rest of this world, the more distance Penny seems to put between us.

We are roommates in Manhattan for only a week when things start to go south. I don't even know exactly what happened. I have been careless. I let little things slip lately. I am rather certain that Penny thinks that I'm either losing my mind or a part of something far too scary for her to fathom.

After I go to see a midnight screening of *Addicted to Love*, I wander back to our place during the wee hours of the morning. Penny is waiting up. She nods at me and looks at me with an intense sort of anger.

There's a feeling of intense dissatisfaction that's shared between the two of us. Although we are best friends, we can no longer talk with the comfortable trust we worked so hard to develop. I know that my secret has been peeling back.

This is what happens when I love. If I allow someone in, while knowing this unknowable secret that I possess, a bar is still up. I am afraid of never sharing true intimacy with friends or anyone else for the rest of my life.

"I was worried about you. Why do you stay out all the time? What's going on? Tell me the truth," Penny begs.

"I always do," I lie.

"You always tell me the truth?"

"I do tell you the truth. I stayed out to see a movie because it's stressful to be around here lately."

"No, I think maybe you've lied to me since the day we met."

"You're paranoid."

As soon as I say that, I regret it. I want to take back the words and swallow them whole. I don't want to force her to take on feelings of inadequacy based on what I can never explain. I vow to myself to never make another false accusation.

"Paranoid, am I? Yeah, right."

Well, at least she's not one for taking on my issues.

"You're my best friend, and you're right. You're not paranoid. I shouldn't have said that. I'm…The truth is that I'm fucked up. I have a lot of…problems. You'd probably be better off if you friend-dumped me."

"Friend-dumped you? What kind of expression is that? Nina, I swear. You're such a weirdo. But don't go overboard. We'll always be friends."

Penny sighs and gets up from the table. She turns and comes back to me.

"Are you pregnant?"

"What? Pen, that's crazy. I haven't even done it."

Of all the things that I worried about coming between us, it's something nonsensical like that? Wow, my mind spins at the superficial binds of what I considered such an important friendship. Is it at risk over some stupid kind of lie?

"I'm going to sleep," I say sadly.

As I walk into my small bedroom, I feel enormously sad. I feel that my most treasured friendship is dying, and the pain feels like it's expanding as I stand there.

I turn on my cell phone to make sure that I didn't miss any messages. I don't actually expect to have any, though, because I am the queen of isolating myself from people I care about. When I hear a message from Leonard explaining that he'd like to see me, I cannot help but let out a little scream of joy.

My door flies open, and Penny stands in the doorway.

"What the hell? Are you okay?" she asks.

"Yeah, sorry. I got a message from the illustrious Mr. Daley," I say.

Penny smiles and nods her head in disbelief. Maybe there is hope for our friendship yet.

Chapter 24 ~ Dated

It turns out that Leonard Daley has lived in New York City for a decade, and he and I only live a few minutes from each other. What a fun connection to have, and I cannot believe how fun it is to spend time with such a fascinating, sensitive person. The more I get to know him, the more I realize how someone so sweet could create art that is sometimes completely unlike himself and, at other times, a seemingly perfect mirror into his soul.

I feel joy as I get ready for my third date with Leonard. We are becoming so familiar with one another, and he seems more interesting with every conversation that we have. It seems to me that most people are more easily understood over time, yet he is still a mystery to me.

When my handsome date and I walk into a homey Italian restaurant together, I feel rather carefree and joyful. We order appetizers and sparkling red wine. I don't like to drink, mainly because I don't want to risk losing control and spilling the secret of my time travel trauma, but the red wine tastes like soda. I figure that I can manage a sip before sticking to the water.

"You know, I've been meaning to tell you. You can call me Lens. My closest friends do," he says, "I prefer that over Lenny, and Leonard just sounds so…formal."

"Okay, Lens."

"What about you?"

"What about me?" I say awkwardly, confirming that I'm the world's worst conversationalist.

"Do you have a nickname?"

"Oh. Right. Yeah, no. I don't. Aside from Pinta and Santa Maria jokes. Um, should I?"

"Not necessarily," he says, and I can tell he's stopping himself from laughing at me.

I take a swig of my sparkling red wine as though it is soda. I'm not sure if it's just the power of what I'm expecting to happen, but I feel a tiny buzz from it almost immediately. I take another drink, then a small sip. Eh, it's okay as far as sparkling wine goes, but I'd rather have some diet soda.

"Here we are! Tada!" the waitress says with great excitement as she sits our green salads down in front of us.

"Thank you," Lens and I say in unison.

"Need anything else now?" she asks sweetly.

I nod, and Leonard says no. She smiles and rushes off. I remember what it was like to be a waitress, so I feel almost guilty when people wait on me. I wish people automatically treated waiters with respect. It has to be among the hardest, most mentally exacting jobs in the world, not to mention one of the most underappreciated.

"So, you're a vegetarian?"

"Yeah, for a long time. If you want to get technical about it, I'm a vegan."

"Is that hard?"

I want to say: *That last word reminds me of something I probably shouldn't be thinking about.* Wisely, I keep my mouth shut and search for an acceptable reply.

"No, not really," I say. "Do you regret asking me for a date?"

"Yeah, that's why I've done so three times now," he says with a sweet sort of sarcasm.

"I…I'm really glad you did."

"The age difference doesn't bother you?"

"There's an age difference?" I smile up at him. "No, it doesn't bother me at all. I haven't really thought about it. Age doesn't seem really important compared to most other things about a person, does it? I think it's weird that people ask each other's ages as if it's not such a temporary aspect of a body that's forever changing."

"It bothered me at first, to tell you the truth, but I think you're really different," he stumbles over his own words.

Lens clears his throat and looks away. I get the idea that he's embarrassed, but I can't fathom why. He usually has all the right words for any situation.

"Different," I repeat, trying to understand if that is a good thing or a bad thing in his eyes.

"You look really beautiful tonight," he tells me what I instantly perceive as a blunt, shallow lie.

"No way," I laugh, "I'm not beautiful, especially compared to the women you know. You've been photographed with supermodels. I'm short. My arms are covered in freckles! Don't try to lie to me."

"I'm not lying. You know, they've done studies on guys who say they like certain things, yet really don't. For men, it's all about trying to impress other guys."

"So, I'm beautiful, but I wouldn't impress your friends?"

"Gah, I've never seen you like this! I was trying to be nice. Honest and nice!" he exclaims, losing just a little of his patience.

"Ah, so I'm a charity case?"

I cringe as I hear myself reply in such a crazy way. Why can't I be quiet? Why must I transform what should have been a sweet moment into something awful? I'm only three dates into this relationship, and my self-sabotage is in overdrive.

Lens pours himself just a tad more wine. However, neither of us care much for drinking at all, so the bottle mostly serves as a table decoration.

My spirit was broken so early in life that I have never recovered. Like horses and other animals that are broken, the imprint of your own frailty and loss stays with you. It's a submissive torment within that feels like your nature because you can't really remember what it was like to be yourself before the hurts began. So you feel that who you really are is a less-than, too-humble being that is willing to do anything to stay in the good graces of those you love, who are clearly superior to you in every way. That's how it is to be tormented as a toddler, to be made to fear and cry for the amusement of the adults around you.

I try to explain this to him, and I start to cry. He grabs me up into his arms and lets me sob on his chest.

"I don't want you to be ashamed of me or think less of me," I confess.

Well, this isn't going well. He already thinks I'm a total mess, and I can just imagine that he's never going to want to see me again. This must be his idea of a date from hell. I want to stop, but I can't seem to do so.

"You *are* beautiful," he says lightly, as though it's just an off-hand comment.

The enormity of that statement strikes me with such force that I become completely overwhelmed. I'm sobbing. I feel myself gasping for breath even. My upper body shakes as sobs rack my body

"Say that again," I manage to whisper.

It's a plea, and it makes me laugh a little inside. Like he's really going to say it again after my initial reaction, but he does. He says it.

"You're beautiful. You really are. Hey, um, why don't we try dancing? I always loved this song."

I listen carefully so that I can discern what song he's enjoying. Then I hear the unmistakably gorgeous tune. Eddie Rabbit and Crystal Gayle are performing on a recording of "You and I," and Leonard twirls me around the dance floor as I savor the loveliness of the music and how he looks in the soft light of the restaurant.

I finally manage to get it together. I hope it's not too little too late, and I vow to myself to be a more fun date next time.

"I'm sorry for the outburst," I say shyly when the song ends.

"Don't be. I can't tell you how refreshing it is to spend time with someone who doesn't feel the need to be fake or put on a show. I wish we all felt comfortable just being who we are and expressing how we feel. I think we'd ultimately all be a lot happier."

Oh, wow. I want to warn him to stop being so wonderful before I fall far more deeply in love with him, but it's too late. It's already happened.

Chapter 25 ~ Clue

On the natural high that being newly in love has given me, I find myself wanting to take a walk. I wander from the small home on Long Island where I'm staying for the weekend just to get away from the stress of living with an increasingly angry Penny. I feel responsible for the problems between us, but I don't know how to stop them.

Before I know it, I've walked all the way to a pier. It's so perfectly beautiful. The only thing that mars the serene vision is the sight of fishermen sitting on the pier; it makes me sick to think of them trying to kill thinking, feeling beings.

The sad scene reminds me of the moment when I became a vegetarian. It was around the time that my dad lost his mind. After he had threatened my life with one of the guns that he used for hunting, I found myself looking into the eyes of the deer heads on the wall. I wanted to tell them that I understood exactly how they felt. I knew what it was like to have my life discounted like it was nothing for the use of a selfish, awful whim.

Even before that day, I always felt much more capable of understanding non-human animals than people. I vowed then to try to protect animals whenever I possibly could.

I always felt such a deep connection to animals. Before I met Lens, I would have sworn that I could never have a similar connection to a fellow human being. To me, animals are as deserving of respect as anyone. Why should we hurt sentient creatures who don't like pain any better than we do?

The presence of the fishermen puts a damper on my glorious mood, and I mosey on over to the swing set. I wipe a tear away as I sit down on a swing in an empty playground along the beach. It's a clear night, and the small, enchanting beach lies just to the right of the pier.

I was looking out at the water when my trance started, and I come out of it when I spot something moving out of the corner of my right eye. I immediately look in that direction, yet I see nothing.

"Hello," I say absentmindedly.

My voice is weak. If someone is there, they are no doubt quick to understand that I'm timid when it comes to encounters with strangers on a nearly deserted beach at night. I laugh at the precarious situation I've put myself in. I stand up and wish I'd driven here instead of walking. I can't bring myself to turn and run; it feels like whoever or whatever is here might take that as an invitation to chase me.

I hear a rustling in the wooden area nearby. How could someone have gotten that far, though? I just saw something from the corner of my eye. It was some speck of lively movement, but whoever was moving didn't take off running for the forest.

"Hello," I say again, finding a more aggressive tone to use.

Now all I hear is radio silence and the rushing of the waves. I force myself to not cut and run. I am accustomed to trusting my instincts, but that hasn't gotten me very far. I decide it's better to ignore my instincts and return to the swing. I start swinging. I go as quickly as I can, pumping my legs so hard that I am practically swinging over the waves themselves.

"You're one of them, aren't you?"

I look up and see a girl who must be around 12 years old just staring at me. She has an outraged expression and eyes that reveal the depths of an old soul. I bring the swing to a stop.

"What?" I ask, internally berating myself for being frightened by a child.

"You know what I mean," she says confidently as she walks to me and takes a seat on the swing next to me. "Race ya?"

The child starts going fast on her swing, so I follow her lead. I take care to go just slower than she does, so that it looks like a fair fight. I have every intention of letting her win, but she slows down at the last second. I find myself speeding past her as she stops and screams at me.

"Congratulations!" she exclaims with a smile.

I stop my swing, too. As I turn to look at her without getting up from my swing, its chains creak and rattle.

"Pretty necklace," she says.

I look down at my necklace. It's the turquoise necklace that Davey gave me. It seems to almost glimmer in the moonlight.

"Thank you. It was a present from my brother. It makes me happy that you mentioned it because I get to think of him an extra time that I maybe wouldn't have today. Thank you."

"You're weird," she says.

"My name's Nina. What's yours?"

"I'm not supposed to talk to strangers," she says coyly.

I look at her with a smile. I know that she's well aware of being the one who approached me.

"Okay, how about we just talk about what you think is going on here?"

"You can call me Susie, and I don't think. I know," she says. "I went back in time. I'm not a child, though."

Oh, shit. For some reason, it didn't sink in until just then that perhaps I really was dealing with someone who was like me. Someone who wasn't a child at all.

"I think I died when I was 37," I say.

"Died? How?"

"Well, I was considering suicide."

"Interesting. I don't think I died at all. I don't think that's when I went back in time. I think I was interrupted on a normal day. I was babysitting my grandkids."

I take in a deep breath. It's unnerving. This woman before me looks so much like a child that all my maternal instincts are kicking in, but she's clearly older than I am.

"Wait a second. So, if you're a child now, and you lived long enough to have grandkids…You've seen a lot further into the future than I did…What's it like?"

"You don't really want to know what it's like, do you? Think about how horrible it is now with no real surprises?"

"Oh, I've had surprises. I never fell truly in love until recently, in this time."

"In this echo," says Susie.

"Echo?"

"Echo. That's what I call what we do. This is my third echo. I've lived four times now. I've only died once. In my first one, I was babysitting the grandkids. I had them again the second time around. Just so you know, death comes unexpectedly. Don't expect to die at one point just because you did in the life before."

"Then how does that work then? If people are going back in time and dying differently, then doesn't that impact the future of everyone else? I mean, at least some of the time?"

"I don't think death is the point at which you went back in time."

"I didn't commit suicide? I really didn't."

Wow, I really didn't. I knew that I didn't remember it. I remember finding such clear hope in the painting of Lens. I had decided to put all notions of ending my life out of my head. Yet, when I woke up as a child, I mostly assumed I must have offed myself, and I'd been so disappointed in myself. The news that this person brings is so freeing that I can't help but give her a big hug.

"That isn't the only thing that you have to worry about, though," she warns. "I think that the cause may be something far scarier than a fluke or a punishment for your sins."

"What do you mean?"

Susie looks around nervously and gets to her feet. She has a look of fear on her face, and she turns to leave.

"Wait," I beg.

Susie hesitates and finally turns around. She looks at me with fear in her eyes.

"Look," Susie says, "I took a big risk to talk to you. Be careful who you trust. Do whatever it takes to stay safe. I have to go now."

"Wait. We have to figure this out. Shouldn't we stick together?"

"No, that's actually the very last thing we should do."

"Why? What the actual fuck?"

"You shouldn't swear in front of children," she says with a smile.

"Answer me this. Have you told anyone? I'm...I really want to tell the man I love."

"Don't. Whatever you do, don't do that. I haven't. Not this echo. Trust me. Don't. I have to go now. Please don't try to find me or contact me. It would just mean big trouble for you."

Susie turns and runs before I have a chance to say anything else. She rushes into the forest that's adjacent to the beach. I feel overwhelmed and like I have a million things to consider all at once. I'm not sure what's going on, but I have even more questions than answers now. Somehow, though, I'm very thankful for this encounter and feel sad that I can't spend more time with Susie. Why did she come to me at all?

I wait on the swing until dawn, hoping Susie will change her mind and come back to me. I suspect that she won't be the only one I meet, and I try to consider that maybe we are all destined to, as she said, "echo" in time. Could that really be God's plan for me? It brings tears to my eyes because I don't want to imagine life without this love that I've just found.

Chapter 26 ~ Harried and Hopeless

Back in Manhattan, as I sit in my kitchen worrying about Susie's fate and my own future, I start distracting myself with thoughts of my past. I think about things in my original life more often than I should. I remember my first boyfriend, and I recall all the verbal abuse he slung at me. That was worse than all the physical abuse that came later when he became my first and only husband.

Knowing that my dad had threatened my life, my then-husband did, too. When I first went to leave him, he terrorized me by grabbing me, pinning me down so I couldn't move, and holding his hand over my mouth and nose. I couldn't breathe. It felt as though it went on for hours, but was probably only a couple of minutes. I felt as though I was truly dying and was about to lose consciousness when he let go just a bit, allowing me to start begging for my life.

Begging for my life was horribly humbling and frightening. I thought: *How terrible and unlovable I am if the two men I loved most in the world tried to kill me?*

Somehow my dad's betrayal had brought out a need for protection, and I felt that need would never be met when I looked into the angry eyes of my former husband. The way he terrorized me broke the fight out of me just enough to scare me from trying to leave.

The degradation and the cruelty went on until I actually begged him to kill me. He'd already made me afraid of my life, so I figured I would rush things along. I wondered if that relationship itself had been a suicide attempt.

After all, I did keep the possibility of suicide in my pocket as a possibility. Had I passively chosen tragedy? I felt that one day, when things got just a little bit worse, I could off myself. When the pain of rejection got just far too heavy to carry, I had a way out. It wasn't if, but when.

Things haven't changed so much. I feel as though the disease of suicide is still surging through my veins, and it's only a matter of time before it ultimately implodes, claiming my life. One thing I can never do, though, is tell someone. It has to be a secret until it's time because I refuse to be the burden my father was.

~

I'm still thinking these things over later in the day when my mind wanders as I sit on the sofa with Lens. We were going to watch a movie, but we quickly grew bored of it and started kissing each other. The passion is growing between us. I pulled away from him to grab something to drink, then came back to sit beside him and rest my head on his shoulder.

While I was gone, he put on a mix CD that I made for him a few weeks ago. We've now gone on so many dates that I've stopped counting them, and there's something so nice about that.

Sitting on the sofa with Lens, it feels like this may be the one time when it's okay to share the problem. Both the suicidal reality of my first lifetime that now feels so much like a dream and my current dilemma of life everlasting.

"Have you ever known anyone who was suicidal?" I dare to ask him.

"Suicidal? Well, I don't know. I mean, it's not the kind of thing people line up to tell you, ya know? I've never been around anyone who threatened suicide. I knew this girl in college…"

I wait about a minute for him to continue the story, but he doesn't. Finally, I lift my head off his shoulder and look at him. He wipes a tear away from his cheek.

"Tell me?" I barely say, too timid to ask him to talk about something so painful. I can't decide whether he wants me to ask and encourage him to share, or if he'd rather I drop the subject. I want to do anything to help soothe his pain.

"Her name was Gabby. She and I went out a couple of times. I didn't think it was a big deal. That's the weird thing. Sometimes feelings can come out of nowhere. Know what I mean?"

I nod. I know exactly what he means somehow.

He continues, "Gabby thought she was in love. For life. With me. And I...didn't want anything heavy. She started talking marriage, so I told her it was over. I didn't think that it had even begun...so saying it was over...that was weird. A couple of nights later she called me in tears. I told her to calm down. I tried to comfort her, but, while we were on the phone, I heard a loud gunshot right at the phone. I called for her, and nothing. I got in my car, rushed over to her place, and I saw her through the window. She'd shot herself; she was gone."

"Oh. Wow. I'm sorry."

"Well, it was so stupid. Such a waste. Maybe she felt all alone or abandoned, I guess, or something. She couldn't have loved me, though. We had just met! So she threw her life away for what?"

I don't have the answers, and I know that nothing I can say will make things better. Instead of trying to speak, I throw my arms around him instinctively, and his head falls onto my chest. I wrap my arm around his head as he allows himself to cry. Once he lets go, he sobs.

I kiss his forehead and caress his cheek. I want to whisper: *There, there.* However, I'm acutely aware that any words would ring out hollow in comparison to the high emotion between us.

As I hold him, I consider how selfish her act was. Yes, it was stupid, but who am I to judge? I never aimed my plans for suicide at anybody, though. I never planned for anyone I loved to find me, and I deliberately distanced myself from people during periods when I became suicidal. I justified these choices because I felt that there was a selfish kind of suicide and an unselfish type; I felt that it was a moral imperative to take the most compassionate path to the end as possible.

To think of this woman hurting Lens made me angry, yet I also felt such sympathy for her. How unbearable it must feel to lose him. After what may have been an hour or only ten minutes, he is still in my arms. He is so still that I wonder if he has fallen asleep for a moment.

"You know," he finally whispers, "I could do this forever. Lie here like this with you."

"Yeah, me too."

"I love you," he says.

I look down at him, and he pulls himself off of me. It feels almost painful to be physically apart because the closeness was so completely soothing. He looks into my eyes with such tenderness, and I think that those eyes must be sore because they are so red.

"I love you," he repeats himself.

I can only take the words in because I can barely breathe. I cannot move or respond. I am shocked.

"I love you," he says a third time.

He kisses me. I start to wonder if the kiss is out of the love he's feeling for me or his need to do something to break me out of my surprised spell. Perhaps he just needs something strong to comfort him tonight. He kisses me long and hard, and it is hard to breathe in the best way.

"I love you, too," I say breathlessly when we finally break apart.

"I want you," I add. I am pretty sure that my voice is incapable of sounding seductive, but I think I got my point across fairly well. I could see both elation and fear cross his face simultaneously. He grabs me at my waist and pulls me up into his lap. As he kisses me, I can feel a tightening and tensing of his body.

"Are you sure you're ready for this?" he asks.

I want it more than I've ever wanted anything. The kiss lulled me into a blissful state where I can't really think of anything else, and the encounter with Susie reminded me of how precious every moment with Lens is. I can't bear to think of ever being parted from this man. I finally get the wherewithal to respond.

"Well," I smile shyly, looking away, "This is earlier than I thought I'd do it."

"We don't have to go through with it," Leonard puts his arms around me as he kisses my forehead lightly. "It's okay. We have all the time in the world as far as I'm concerned. I'm not going anywhere."

I get lost in memories of what was supposed to be a romantic wedding night. After I married my ex, that night wasn't the romantic dream I hoped it would be. I remember the pain and disappointment when it seemed that my own husband didn't want me. I felt like the only married woman who had no idea what sex felt like. I was utterly humiliated. Life seemed to be a series of ongoing rejections. I find myself feeling really angry. My body hadn't been worthy then, and I feared that it wouldn't be now.

I am brought back to reality as Lens wraps his arm around me. We come together again. When he puts his hands on me, I suddenly realize that I may be in way over my head. No matter how old I may be mentally, this is a bit much for me. I haven't had sex after all this time, and I wonder what it will be like.

Once again, the memories of my past come back to haunt me. I smile at him, resting my head on his shoulder.

"Let's not decide tonight," I say gently.

"Okay."

"It's just that I can't," I whisper.

I am mad because I want to do it as much as I'm a little afraid of what it will actually be like. Am I losing my mind? Maybe that's what all this is! All these years of indulging my total insanity. They must have put me in a madhouse, and that's why I am having this grand, long delusion. It must be it. How else could I possibly be turning down Lens?

"You can't?" he asks tenderly.

Oh, no. He looks at me as though he is totally and completely dumbfounded. What have I done?

"I'm a virgin," I say with a wave of my hand. "I mean, I'm sure I can figure out…I'm a fast learner…I just mean…"

Although I cannot seem to form an articulate sentence, I'm otherwise amazed at my self-control. It's comfortable to hang out with him and feel no pressure. Instead of getting mad, he reaches over and kisses me again.

"No worries. Let's just talk. I love hanging out with you," he says.

The compliment just doesn't fit. I try to accept it, and it makes me squirm. I'll never not be the fat girl in my head. I earned her. She protected me.

To compound matters and make me feel even worse, I feel stupid for the private thoughts in my own head because so many fat women are absolutely gorgeous. To tell you the truth, I think everyone is beautiful, but I'll never allow myself to be in that group. I am decidedly ugly, and that's how I see myself. The compliment feels nice anyway, though.

I actually stop thinking about myself long enough to consider what his feelings could be. I think about him and his feelings more often when we're not together. However, when Lens and I are actually together, I find myself trying to be someone better than myself to somehow impress him. It's an odd circle of selfishness and self-loathing.

"When did you know that you wanted to be an artist?" I ask him.

I'm very interested in his answer. I want to know everything about him. Any fact about his life simply fascinates me. He leans back and looks as though he's deep in thought. Leave it to him to give any question the proper amount of consideration that a good answer requires.

"I don't think I ever had a big aha moment. It was just always part of what I did. I had to express myself through creating. I drew on everything in sight, and I'd wear down all the markers in the house by using them as sort of makeshift paintbrushes. I started painting with oils when I was around 12 or so."

"That's amazing," I say honestly. "I want to see everything you've ever done."

"Well, I don't know about that, but I can show you some stuff I've done recently."

I kiss him, and I grab him in my arms. It's just such a beautiful night for talking and feeling.

Chapter 27 ~ This Love

Hope was the most powerful emotion I ever felt until I met Leonard. Now that I know him, I cling to hope more than ever, but the love I feel for him has become the ever-present force in my life. In fact, the love I feel is still changing me completely. It shifts and pushes the edges of my true self, nudging me to be better and forcing me to be more honest about what the hell really matters anyway.

I like being on my own. I never wanted or needed a boyfriend. I enjoy going to the movies by myself and sitting right in the front row like unsupervised kids do. I like pigging out on chocolate-covered peanuts and extra-large cokes without worrying about what some man thinks about my body. I don't get lonely when I'm on all-day excursions on my own, and I don't long to have company on quiet weekends. I take complete care of myself. However, I've finally found a man that I want, even if I don't need anyone at all.

Sometimes when I watch him cross the room, or when I turn around to look at him when he laughs while I am at the stove, at first glimpse, he looks like someone beyond a mere mortal. I know he is a human being, but he seems like a being made of light and crystal and warmth. He seems so filled with a sort of peace and ease that I don't yet understand.

Our first month together flows by in flashes of joy, affection, and excitement. It's rare for a wish fulfilled to be better than its anticipation, but the time I spend with Leonard is far better than I thought it would be. Where I imagined fun, we have ecstasy. Although I expected to lose a part of myself in a passion this intense, I find that I'm feeling stronger and more fulfilled. I still brace myself for rejection at every turn, afraid that this is too good to be true, but I keep finding new reasons to trust him and relax.

None of our differences matter at all anymore. Besides, we're alike in more ways than anyone would guess from our circumstances. I tell him about everything except the echo of that other life that still haunts me, the other one where he didn't, in fact, want me. A part of me needs to tell him about even that, but nobody would believe me; that's a lesson I have to carry alone. So I block it out as best I can and try to live only in the present.

Although we still haven't made love, I think of being with him in every possible way each time that I see him. I went two weeks without any food at all when I was first twelve years old, and eventually the fierce hunger sort of tapered down to a steady ache.

The desperate longing I feel for Lens is far more intense than a mere hunger for food, and it hasn't eased up even a tiny bit, not in all this time. Now that he's here, so close and actually with me, it keeps growing. Sometimes I feel like it's going to completely overwhelm me, and maybe I'll implode from the heat.

Kissing has become a familiar state of euphoria that he and I share nearly every day. No matter what kind of date we have, we end up at his house or my apartment with our lips joined and our arms around one another. He's patient and sweet, letting me set the pace for how fast we take things. I love him so much that I want more than I can ask for, yet tonight I feel like my desires are taking over.

I knock on my own bedroom door. Lens has been in there disrobing. I asked him to come over tonight to be my guinea pig. I took an online massage course ages ago, and I've been dying to try out the skills I supposedly learned.

"Ready?" I ask expectantly.

"Um, yeah," I hear him say a bit meekly.

As I walk into the room, he is lying face down on the bed. His head rests on a pillow, and he has pulled a towel over his naked body. I am tempted to pull it off and seduce him here and now. Instead, I remind him to relax and breathe deeply as I try to do the same.

The plan for tonight is to excite and satisfy all of his senses, starting with his sense of smell. The aroma of the lit vanilla candles fills the air, and I pour lavender-scented massage oil on both hands. For his listening pleasure, I have a romantic mix CD playing songs I know he enjoys, starting with "Through the Eyes of Love".

As far as sight goes, I have the room decorated as elegantly as I can. The candles cast shadows that ebb and flow, and their soft light makes the room glow. I wear a satin, navy blue nightgown in an attempt to be beautiful. Even after all this time, I cannot believe that this thin, muscular body is my own now, but I never hesitate to dress it up.

Now for touch! My hands caress his shoulders and work their way firmly over his muscles, and the heat from his body makes me blush. Suddenly a knock on my front door startles us both, and he turns to his side in a knee-jerk reaction. The towel falls aside, and I see his erection. Instead of looking away, I study his body, and he doesn't move.

There is no way that I am going to answer the door and let anyone intrude on our night, so I ignore it. I can't seem to peel my eyes away from him, and he smiles.

"Tell me what's on your mind," Leonard says, softening his eyes in a way that makes me want to kiss his long eyelashes as they beat down softly on his cheeks.

"I'm ashamed of how turned on I am by you right now," I whisper.

"Don't be," he matches my soft tone. "I want you."

His lips find mine, and I pull myself onto the bed. It's not enough to simply be beside him, though.

"Lens, I want you, too," I say boldly as I run my hands through his hair.

"Are you sure you're ready?"

I nod yes, and our hands are quickly exploring each other. My gown is over my head in a moment, and I toss it to the ground. I am wearing nothing underneath, and I gasp at this realization. It's hard not to feel the old self-loathing that follows me and taunts me from the corners of every room I enter, but I'm quickly distracted by such acceptance and pleasure that the thoughts shut themselves up.

"You're beautiful," he whispers.

I was just thinking the same thing about him. My hands need to touch every part of his body, and I leave a trail of kisses up and down his chest. His eyes close as I restlessly touch his thighs, then his arms encircle me, bringing me to his chest in a sweet embrace. The closeness intensifies the heat between us and the fervor I think we're both feeling.

Lens takes my hands and pins me to the bed as we kiss, and I feel complete trust in his power over me. He moves my legs apart with his own, and I close my eyes as he pushes himself into me. The initial pain gives way to pleasure as we find a perfect rhythm together. I thrust my hips up to meet his body, and I feel a profound satisfaction as our eyes meet. We whisper about our deepest feelings for one another as my body adjusts to his. So this is making love.

Chapter 28 ~ Deserving

Making love last night was something beautiful and as sacred a thing as I'd ever experienced. I'd always imagined it happening on my wedding night, yet it was far more intense than I'd dreamed it would be even within a commitment as deep as marriage. It seemed a rash decision under the cover of darkness, but, in the clarity of the afterglow, it feels like the perfect decision was made. I am overwhelmed by how attracted I am to him.

I think but dare not say: *I could die happy, but now I want to live forever.*

All the things I want to say seem stupid and cheesy, but I don't care at all. I feel utterly silly and giddy with love. The spiritual intimacy between us seems to be stronger after our lovemaking. It was there to begin with, and making love seems to have magnified all the beauty that was already going on between us.

The more I learn about Lens, the more enchanted I am with him. We talk about everything. He whispers his secrets in my ear while we cook, shop, or just dance around the living room to our favorite songs. We explore museums, and I slowly come to learn how he became such an incredible artist, even while the man he is still remains a bit mysterious.

He and I go on road trips to theme parks, enjoy picnics in the car on deserted mountain roads, and explore some haunted houses even though neither of us believes in ghosts. We're pretty much up for anything and just having adventures as fast as we can find things to share with each other. We start with a little bit of time together, then it seems that we are spending each and every day by one another's side.

I talk to him about the past, unable to stop myself. Leonard tells me that the bad things that happened to me in the past aren't my fault. That I didn't deserve the horrible things that have happened, yet he also assures me that I do deserve the good things now. Nobody told me anything like that before, and his compassion and kind words really dig deep and comfort me.

I am feeling perfect bliss. Occasionally I'll get the feeling that we are being watched, or I look across the room right as someone looks quickly away. Certainly it is just paranoia, my own sordid imagination, and I don't let anything interfere with the fun I'm having.

I'd never been able to stop considering what the right thing to do was, but it suddenly doesn't matter to me when it comes to being with him. The euphoria of finally being so close to someone like him becomes all that matters to me in each instant. I still care deeply for others, but I let myself get carried away in the passion I feel.

How can you turn things around so completely and become someone entirely different from the person you were yesterday? I don't know. I don't care. All I know is that I have to be with him as much as I possibly can. I don't care what I have to give up and what sacrifices need to be made from me or anybody else. I'm sorry, and I'm not at all sorry. I am in love.

Chapter 29 ~ Surprise

When it goes on for a long time, it's far too tempting to lose yourself in a love that's as all-encompassing as the one I feel for Lens. I could have locked myself up in a tower with him and never even missed the world at large.

If I'd managed to squeeze out a largely selfless existence at some points in my life, I was incapable of doing anything of the sort now. That's not to say that I lost myself. I simply discovered how deeply I was capable of loving another human being; it rocked me to my core.

That kind of love can survive, but it has to get more flexible as it grows stronger. Otherwise, it becomes unhealthy and only sustainable at an unbearable expense to the two people who love so strongly.

Now I sit in the kitchen as I plan Leonard's birthday surprise. I want to give him the most memorable birthday of his life. I don't know what he would appreciate when it comes to material things. No matter how much time I spend with him, I cannot get close enough to him to satisfy the longing that still burns within me for him.

I'm lost in thought, and I don't notice when he walks in.

"What's the matter with you?" he asks.

I jump a bit from the shock, then laugh it off. I smile at him. I wish I could answer that with a simple word or even a paragraph of run-on sentences. What is the matter with me cannot be summed up in a way that I dare to speak. For a moment, though, I am tempted to tell him about that one time I somehow traveled back through time itself, and somehow, this time around, I found the most wonderful love with him.

"Oh, nothing. What are you doing?"

"Looking at you and thinking about last night," he says with that sweet spark in his eyes.

"We could recreate it by daylight," I suggest. "I always liked reruns. There's something to be said about knowing what to expect."

"I usually prefer surprises, but I think I'll make an exception."

I put my arms around his waist and pull him towards me, feeling as though I have to kiss him in this very moment, or I will just die.

Chapter 30 ~ The Best Part

I decide that the birthday surprises for Lens will be simple, and they'll last throughout the week. I start by bringing him breakfast in bed on Sunday. I feel like I'm doing a good job of making him happy as I put the tray full of all his favorite breakfast foods on his lap along with my own specialty: a tofu scramble.

"What do you like best?" he asks as he looks over at me while I take a seat on the bench beside the bed.

"About a tofu scramble?"

"Sex. About sex. Having sex with me."

"Oh, that." I say with a smile, "Well, aside from the high of seeing you experiencing pleasure as I'm feeling it..."

I find myself embarrassed and unable to go on, not quite wanting to tell him. How ridiculous, I chide myself. How is it that I can be so intimate and open with this man, yet not want to answer such a simple question?

"Oh, come on. Now you have to tell me. I'll start. I like the way that it feels to share the closeness on every level. Like...it brings it all together. That sounded better in my head, but ya know..."

"I feel that, too. The best part for me is how I feel like I belong to you. When we make love...it feels like...It's so mind-bending and different from anything else I've known. It's exciting."

I expect him to judge that for some reason. I'm judging my own self for being silly and stupid. Before I can look up, I feel his arms around me. He's behind me, with one arm over my shoulders as his elbow touches my right breast. His other arm grabs my waist. He kisses my neck sweetly and gently.

"You do belong to me, and I belong to you," he whispers. "Those are my other favorite parts."

I moan as I realize that I'm about to spend the morning in bed reliving our favorite parts.

Chapter 31 ~ Story Love

Being in love in Manhattan intensifies everything I love about the City That Never Sleeps. In addition to all the artistic glory that the city holds, there's something magical about sharing such a strong intimacy that only he and I understand while we are among millions. We stroll down the busy streets in November, which is the time of year when the city's edgy beauty seems amplified.

I stop at a crosswalk in front of Macy's and look at the beautiful window displays. The severe winter wind blows my hair off my shoulders. I watch the loose strands dance in the wind and realize that I haven't washed my long mane in a couple of days. I've been so preoccupied with the wonder of Lens that I haven't thought of things like washing my hair or even brushing the lint off my coat, and the neglect makes me laugh.

"What's so funny?" Lens asks as he wraps his arms around me.

"What's not? Everything feels like Christmas."

I kiss him as pedestrians push past us. The streetlight must have changed, but I am totally uninterested in anything except for Lens. No matter what their intentions may be, angry passersby are only doing me a favor when they push me even closer to my man. I maneuver our way through the crowd with a smile.

"We better get going. We're going to miss the show," Lens finally says with a slight laugh.

As he hesitantly pulls away from my eager kisses, he loses this round of ignore-the-world. It's a game we play all the time these days.

Nothing else really matters now that we have each other, and we have created our own little blissful bubble in which we can dwell and adore each other.

His large hands cover both of mine as he walks behind me. Our fingers are intertwined, and it's a fun way to go through the bustling city. Although the streets in this part of Manhattan are overly crowded nearly any time of day, I know better than anyone how utterly lonely they can feel. It's a euphoric rush to know a togetherness so unique that loneliness now seems preposterous.

As I order our tickets for the movie, Lens goes to get popcorn, candy, and Cokes. Health food be damned, we're out for some fun before we go back to our place for pleasure. The line is huge for both films, but that's what you get when you go see a big blockbuster flick.

He puts his right arm around me as we sit down in the theater. As I look over at him, I think: *Mad, unconditionally true love is ridiculous.* There is nothing about it that makes any sense at all, and any attempt at normalizing it is stupid. Worse yet, trying to make it fit into the box of ordinary, everyday love will do no good. It must simply stand alone in the way that it joins two people together and be a force that leads the way. All I know is that I'm in it, and I'd do anything in the world for him.

Chapter 32 ~ Best Laid Plans

Lens invites me to his house on Long Island. As I pull up in his driveway, the cold has lessened with the heat of the sun that seems to be causing the asphalt to sizzle. I get out of my rental car, locking the doors, and I think to myself that I'd never have imagined that it was so cold just a couple of hours ago.

When I step out of my car, though, I see that the frigid temperatures are quickly making a comeback. I open my cell phone and give it a voice command to call Lens as I knock. He doesn't answer his phone or the door. Puzzled, I call again, and I knock harder. No luck! I jump when I feel someone touch my shoulder, and I start to scream. My scream is interrupted by a laugh of relief when I realize that it's Lens.

"Don't sneak up on me like that," I half-scold while I laugh along with him.

"Honestly, I didn't mean to," he lies, and we both know it.

I kiss him anyway. I kiss him again. We embrace, kiss, and talk as we somehow make our way inside. It's as warm inside as it is cold outside, and I love the idea of being in the house that Lens chose. I want to discover what it is he that he loves about it.

Talking with him is so easy that I completely relax. I forget all the fear that I clasp far too often. In fact, I usually keep the fear wrapped around me like a blanket so that I don't slip and reveal some future reference from my first life. With him, there seems to be no need of it. His gentle behavior moves me, and he strikes me as someone who'd understand a slip-up. He's everything I never imagined it was possible for a man to be.

I look at his home, and I marvel at how perfectly suited to him it is. I go to the kitchen and almost gasp because I've never seen one quite so homey and perfect; it feels like you just want to hang out in it for hours at a time. The kitchen is decorated in baby blue and pastel peach, with blue roses in an ornate peach vase by the windowsill beneath lace curtains.

"Did you decorate your house yourself?" I ask.

"Yeah, if you can call it decorating," he says humbly.

The way that he looks down and then up to smile at me is beautiful. I'm tempted to say: *Stop being so perfect.*

With this enchanting Victorian home, he created a haven for himself where he can relax and enjoy a serene getaway. Only a few minutes pass before I'm focused on Lens again, though, and not so much on his house.

We find our way to his bedroom. I lie under his arms. I feel his breath against my skin, and every time he exhales I feel surges of warmth and wonder. Being this close to Lens feels permanent, although I fear that it may be temporary. I won't let myself believe that he loves me or that this can work out. To do so and lose him would be impossible, so I brace myself for the inevitable separation while savoring every second that I do have with him. In this moment, I am good enough.

Lying in wonder, I somehow fall asleep. When my eyes open, nightfall is upon us, and I find Leonard's beautiful brown eyes looking at me. I gasp in shock and excitement. He laughs, and I can't help but join in.

"That time, I didn't mean to scare you. For real."

"No, you didn't. I'm not scared."

I wonder how many times we can possibly squeeze making love in one lifetime. I want to constantly bring him pleasure. I kiss him. We must make love again, or I think I'll burst. Then suddenly he's above me, and we're moving together as though we are one.

I wake up, and he is holding me. Life feels absolutely perfect. He talks to me, and I try to pay attention. However, all I can really do is think about how pleasurable every part of his skin feels against mine.

Chapter 33 ~ Day Mare

I walk through Leonard's neighborhood; it's still unfamiliar. I come across a park. It's gated, but I have the key. The sun is rising, and the winds blowing. It's just warm enough that the cool winds feel heavenly as they blow across my cheeks.

I hear the creaking of a swing and realize that I'm not alone in the park. I look over and see a woman pushing a child on a swing. I get closer because I want to say hello, but there's a tragic, pained look in the woman's eyes. She won't make eye contact with me, and I look away feeling a bit embarrassed. When I look back in her direction, I noticed her little girl's eyes are wide open and vacant. The child is dead.

I scream. I find myself waking up in bed. I'm only silently screaming in reality. Oh, it was only a dream. The sense of dread is still with me. My heart races, and I try to remember the breathing technique that I once learned in a fusion yoga class to slow my heart rate. It's no use, though. I've forgotten that and everything else I attempted to learn in all the hundreds of exercise classes I've taken.

I just lie there like a blob as my heart pounds. I surrender to the fear, and I find myself slowly calming down. Maybe that's the secret to all these echoing lives. Something feels really off today, though, and I pull myself up in bed. Looking at the clock on the floor, I think of all the things I have to do today. It's already six in the morning, so there's no point in trying to get back to sleep now and risk another nightmare. I'm up for the day.

Scary happens. I need to just get over it.

Chapter 34 ~ Windfall

Lens and I have been together for over a year now, and I don't want it any other way. It's only October, but the wind swirls around me. An indefinable cold suddenly permeates my body, and it feels like the dead of winter. I walk a little faster. Something's wrong. It's not that exactly. It's more like I can tell that not everything is just as right as it should be. I can't put my finger on what's off, but that doesn't make it any less true.

I'm not really worried because my mind is in the clouds, dreaming of Lens. I get so lost in thoughts of the most recent night we spent intertwined that I'm startled when I hear a Madonna tune; it takes me a half-second to realize that it's the ringtone I've heard a million times on my phone.

"Hi," I say, tossing the phone to my ear without looking to see who is calling.

"Nice red shoes," an unfamiliar voice on the line says flatly. "Where are you going in such a hurry?"

Instantly startled and frightened, I stop. I look down at my red Keds; they match my red dress. I pull the phone out and see that this call is from an "Unknown Number". I look around me. The white picket fence to my left and the two-story Victorian to my right don't seem to be hiding suspicious characters. I am getting rather familiar with the Long Island neighborhood that Lens calls home.

How could anyone be watching me? The wildflowers of fall make the street seem undeniably cheery, and so do the gardens within the carefully manicured lawns that run up and down both sides of the street. Squirrels play together just ahead of me. What is going on?

"What?" I finally say, "Lens, this isn't funny."

I hope and pray that it is Lens playing some kind of practical joke, though I know that is something he'd never do. He could never truly frighten me on purpose. He'd be angry at anyone who dared to seriously scare me.

"Lens? What kind of a name is that? Is that your pet name for Mr. Daley?"

My heart jumps into my throat. This stranger knows about my Lens. I twirl around, paying attention as best I can to the world around me, looking for anywhere someone may be hiding.

"Who is this?" I shout. "Where are you?"

"Now, now. Stop twirling. You're making me dizzy."

I hang up the phone and race down the street. I'm terrified. I don't see anyone out aside from a child who's walking a Great Dane that rivals her in height. The little girl certainly wasn't making the phone call.

When I get home, I'm too terrified to go inside alone. I bring my phone to my ear as I press the instant call button for Lens.

"Hey, sweetheart," he says.

"Where are you? How fast can you get home?"

I hear the front door open, and I turn around as my heart pounds. I was afraid of seeing the stranger, but instead it's Lens. He's home. Thank God. I run into his arms and let my fearful tears flow freely.

Chapter 35 ~ Hot Shot

Lens and I are intimate as soon as we are inside the house, and somehow it certainly calms me down. In fact, I am feeling downright giddy when Lens brings us tea for two in bed. I stretch out and luxuriate in the feeling of being so deeply in love, and it's hard to deny that I am loved as deeply as I love.

As Lens returns with tea, I look at the clock and see that it's only noon. We have much of the day to spend together, and I'm savoring the idea of free time spent in his company.

"I just got a message from Jocasta. We have to head back into the city."

Jocasta handles the selling of Leonard's original works of art. It pains me that he sells his artwork because I love it all. I could just climb into each painting and feel perfectly content to stay in that beautiful world forever. The idea of going back into the city when I planned on having Lens all to myself certainly does not thrill me. However, since I know that it's for his art, I quickly agree that we should.

A night of networking at a big art gallery is a bit exhausting. The event is an impromptu showing of the work of multiple artists, and so many people want to meet Lens. They seem totally disappointed to see me in his presence. I don't mind because I'm so very proud of him. I don't hate it when it's time to go, though.

Lens takes me to a beautiful restaurant, and we celebrate the end of the evening. Neither of us are really excited about the idea of trying to sell things to strangers. Lens is excited by the creation of art, not selling it, and I understand his passion.

We are relieved that the show is over. Lens feels comfortable enough to start teasing me about how frightened I got by the prank call from the stranger. He assures me that it really is nothing.

"Keep talking. Go on as if I'm listening to a word you're saying. Just keep talking. Yet you should know that the grin on your face tells me everything," I say to tease him.

His grin reveals that he likes my odd kind of humor. As he excuses himself to go to the bathroom, I look more closely at the menu. It doesn't hold my attention for long, though, because I can't help but look up at the beautiful restaurant that we're in.

The formal Italian restaurant has a winter wonderland theme, with the most elegant display of white and light blue lights. The owner of the restaurant has spared no expense in creating an ambiance that's equal parts romantic and festive. A small, live band plays magical sounds, and a small dance floor tempts me.

"Can I admit now that I was a nervous wreck? I hate black tie business bullshit," he says mischievously.

I look up at him as he sits back down beside me. I wish that I was as tall as he is, and I wish that I formed and expressed opinions as easily as he does.

"I don't know what's sadder. That I enjoy dressing up a bit too much, or that we both walked around the gallery all night without eating the food."

"Networking, sweetheart. Since we got that corporate annual hell over for the year, I feel much better, though. Don't you? I just want to focus on creating art now, not selling it. Oh, and on our dinner here now that it's just us."

I nod and smile.

"You were amazing tonight with that crowd," I say.

He nods, but I can tell that he's dismissing my opinion as though it doesn't even matter. I wonder why he seeks validation from other people, but my opinion as a person doesn't seem to amount to much of anything at all. Maybe I'm just misreading a simple motion.

Suddenly the orchestra starts to play "You and I," a song that I never hear any more. I can't help that a squeal of delight escapes from my gut.

"Our song! Did you tell them to play that?"

"I just might know someone who knows someone..."

"That's all you're saying?"

"That's all I'm saying. You know, I think we have a few minutes before the entrees arrive."

"Why, yes, you may have this dance!"

He handles me gently as we dance.

He whispers, "I'll never forget the first time we danced to this. I was actually nervous, and I don't get scared. Then I felt your heartbeat going even faster than mine. That's the only way I knew you were nervous, too. You looked calm and elegant, though. I don't know how you kept it together."

"I still get all excited dancing with you."

I rest my head on his shoulder as we slow dance. All feels right with the world. It feels more than alright when he kisses my neck just a bit as we dance.

"Will you promise me things will always be just like this?"

I am needy. People always tell me not to be needy; they fuss at me for being who I naturally am. I should be better and stronger. I am independent, but what's the proper amount of independence? What's healthy and what's not? Is it not a sort of spectrum that's different for everyone?

"I promise things will only get better from here. We're going to build a life so amazing that it will completely make up for everything horrible that ever happened to you," he says gently.

"I hope you're happier than I am because I feel completely euphoric," I reply.

~

He and I lie in bed. Arms and legs intertwine, and I feel all tangled up with him. It feels beautiful. We're also a bit entangled with our aquamarine Egyptian cotton sheets. He kisses my neck as I lie beside him looking at the ceiling in a sort of awed tiredness.

Tears start to well in my eyes, and that alarms Leonard. He swings his body around the bed so that he's looking into my eyes.

"Hey, hey, hey there. What is it?" he asks gently.

"You know, I try to see things through your perspective. And I can't help but think, you must think it's so hard to have such an emotional partner. Do you ever just wish you could blink and be with someone less complicated? You must hate having to deal with me."

"I don't hate having to deal with any part of you at all. It's more like the opposite. For starters, I love having to deal with your passion."

He reaches down and kisses me.

"It's not too out of control for you?"

"Not a chance. I also love dealing with the way you are the most compassionate person I know."

"Really?"

"Yeah, I never knew anybody so full of compassion. I also love having to deal with the fact that I just know you'd do anything for me."

"I really would."

"I'd do anything for you, too."

He kisses me again.

"What about my body?"

"I love dealing with your body more than just about everything else. I have to be real about that, right?"

He grins as he starts to lean in for another kiss.

Chapter 36 ~ The Ugly Shade of Green

My worries sometimes center on the strange girl who came to me at the beach and the man who seems to oddly walk in my life at random times. I laugh it off, though, chiding myself for making something out of nothing. Whatever it is that happened to me may be just a fluke, and the blessings I have now are more than I dared to even want in my first life. I try to make that enough, but I wish I could share this secret with my love.

The things that are on my mind are never ones I'd have chosen. I'm giving valuable, prime real estate within me to all the horror I hate. I realize that in one sickening swirl of the way I feel. It's only when I'm with Lens that I feel focused on the things I love instead, and he moves to the center of all I love.

Five blissful years with Lens seem to pass so quickly that I start to get scared. I want to slow time down. Even though I seemingly have so much time now, I can't be certain. I don't feel that any length of time is guaranteed, and I find myself wanting so very much to live forever now that I'm feeling so happy.

A high level of happiness means that you have a lot to lose, though, and I get very protective of what I share with Lens. The jealousy increases, and I fear that makes the joy we're experiencing decrease. Although I rarely act in jealousy, I very much feel it, and its very existence has a way of spreading poison around.

I still think of Penny. Our friendship was so important, and we were so close. Then she just seemed to want to fade from my life. I fought for our friendship in my own way, and maybe she did in her own way. It just wasn't enough, and I miss her. I don't ever want to know what it's like to miss Lens on a long-term basis. Just the pang of missing him for a day is already intolerable.

I wake up on a Tuesday morning in August of 2001. I've been starting to worry so much about the horrors that were experienced during my first life in the upcoming month. I don't know what I can do to make things better. I've been worried about all the tragedies and needless deaths around the world, so I try to act in the most effective ways and do the most good I can for others.

I am clueless about what could stop the attacks. Surely, if I change the particular planes or manage to shut down whole airports, then those responsible will just find another way. I feel so much for the families who lost loved ones, and I don't know what to do.

I feel paralyzed by fear, and something distracts me. I hear Lens talking on the phone in our bathroom. I hear him talking so sweetly that I wonder if maybe he has decided that I am unworthy after all. I tell myself that's an utterly unreasonable direction for my mind to travel, but it's already left the train station and is barreling full force ahead.

I feel like I will never be able to stop wondering what I should be doing instead of the action I'm actually completing in each moment. I cannot sit idly by while known disasters occur, can I? Yet, what if preventing one thing leads to something even more tragic? How do you choose to save some people when new ones will be destroyed in their place?

I suddenly have a compulsion to hurt myself. I have enough perspective to realize that is merely a fleeting feeling, and it's not something I really need to actually do at all. For the moment, though, the pain explodes over and over again. I let it.

In the next moment, Lens comes out of the bathroom with his phone in hand. He looks over at me and smiles, looking genuinely happy to see me awake.

"Who was that?" I ask.

"Jocasta. She has some new ideas for promoting the exhibit," he says, referring to a new art show that's featuring his work in Manhattan.

"Oh" I say, "Why were you talking to her in the bathroom, instead of out here?"

"Because I didn't want to wake you up. You were sleeping so soundly, and you've earned the right to sleep in, ya know?"

Lens is so considerate that I feel even worse for my negative thoughts. He quickly distracts me as he starts telling me about an idea he has for a new painting that stems from that time when he was a kid when he first discovered how to write music.

"Am I boring you?"

He asks me that ridiculous question, and I want to answer it in such a passionate way.

I say, "No, not at all."

What I want to say is: *Every word you utter is magically beautiful to me. You are the most fascinating man I've ever known.*

"I can't wait to see your work on display at the opening. I'm just a little scared. I tend to feel like people want me to disappear at those things," I say, then want to bop myself over the head for such selfish thoughts.

"If anyone's rude to you, I'll hurt them," Lens tells me.

"I've never heard you threaten violence before," I laugh.

Chapter 37 ~ Tragedy

I couldn't live with myself if I did nothing. I had to at least try to stop the horrible goings-on of the terrorist attacks in September 2001. So on September 1, I made my way to a public library on Long Island, deliberately taking the Long Island Railroad to a random stop where I didn't think anyone would recognize me. I ducked into a library and used the computer without signing in.

Worried that my emails would probably be dismissed as the talk of a crazy person by most people, I made sure to send them to senators, the President, the FBI, and anyone else that I could possibly contact online who I felt could have any influence or major interest. I copied and pasted a simple email begging them to stop the attacks and giving them any details I could remember.

After I discreetly wiped my prints from the computer, I rushed out of the place and ran to get on the train that was destined for Manhattan. I hoped and prayed that nobody would notice me on the ride, so I tried my best to act natural.

My fears were realized when the towers collapsed all over again. It was heartbreaking. I couldn't bear to see people relive the horror. It was horrible to think of little children living through such great losses again. I had failed. I felt as guilty and responsible as I did when Dad killed Mom and Davey.

I feel the world closing in. Tears won't stop falling. I've been crying all day, and the pain stabs at my eyes. Every time I close them, it's as though the tears left behind razor blades on the insides of my eyelids. Every blink hurts me to the core, where I'm already writhing in pain.

Now I sit looking outside the window of the home I now share with Lens. I see two police cars out front, and I find myself wondering if maybe my emails had been received after all. With so many people being forewarned, why had they done nothing? It occurred to me that I might be required to pay a huge price for trying to prevent the attacks.

I notice two detectives get out of their cars and go to my front door.

"Lens!" I scream.

"What is it?" he asks as he rushes into the room.

"There are police out front," I say.

"What? That's not funny. What are you up to?"

"I'm serious, and I think they're here for me."

As if on cue, there is a loud knocking on our front door.

"Here for you? What did you do, smooth criminal?" he says teasingly.

"I tried to stop something horrible from happening."

"Something horrible? You're not talking about…"

The attacks are on everyone's mind, so that's what he thinks about first. People all over the country have changed so much within this month.

"I didn't do anything wrong," I repeat, "Please don't lose faith in me."

I rush to the door and let the detectives take me away for questioning.

Chapter 38 ~ Confusion

Lens drives me home with a broken expression on his face. My questioning is over, and nothing terrible is happening to me because it's clear that I did nothing wrong. That doesn't mean the detectives still aren't very suspicious of me, and it doesn't mean that Lens hasn't started to fear the worst about me.

It's not about finding happiness in life as much as it is about creating it for myself and maybe even more about making others happy. I mean, even though it feels more and more temporary. I want to bring joy to Lens, and I start to fear that I may never be able to do so again.

All of a sudden reality starts to set in. Well, I realize that I don't know reality at all. We are familiar only on the most superficial level. It also hits me that I totally messed up. All the potential that I had seems wasted. I managed to ruin all the chances that I had for something so wonderful and beautiful.

It's not fair to me or Lens, but I start to wonder whether he has been waiting for me to screw up so that he could leave me without any guilt. I feel disposable, like I was someone that he wasted time with while waiting for someone far more special and deserving of his love. This one hurts, and I hope that this awareness comes to an end once and for all. Going through this pain every day for the rest of my life is unfathomable. I can barely get through this minute.

Anger simmers beneath the surface of my feelings. I love this man more than anything, and I want nothing more than to make things work. I know that I'm losing him, though. He's slipping from my fingers. The more passionately I try to hold on, the more unstable my grasp becomes.

"You don't trust me," I say as Lens turns into our neighborhood.

"What? How could you say that?"

"You don't trust me. I see it in your eyes. You have no idea how much that hurt."

"You scared me."

"You scared me," I answer quietly.

"Don't do this to us," he says.

"I'm not doing it," I cry.

"Hey, hey," he whispers in a protective tone. "I'm sorry."

"What the hell are you sorry for?"

My anger is at the boiling part, and I cannot explain why. He's told me not to do this, so clearly he thinks that I am to blame for our coming undone. I tried everything I knew how to do. I want to stay together at all costs, but apparently I've failed. I want to know what I did that was so wrong, but I suddenly find myself unable to form words around the man who has become the center of my world.

"Geez, I'm just sorry that…"

"That I failed you?"

"You didn't fail me," I reassure him.

Okay, so there it is. We both feel like we're letting each other down. We're angry. So how is it that we can't work things out? Why do I feel that we're doomed, no turning back?

"I wish I knew what to do," he says. "This shouldn't be happening."

"It's not just happening. We're both making choices. It's all about what we choose to do. I gotta say, I'm still choosing you. I want to be with you."

We're home, and he pulls the car into the driveway. He stops and pulls the key out of the ignition. He makes no move to get out of the car, though.

"I want to be with you," I repeat, and I start going a bit numb to survive the crushing pain when he doesn't say the same thing to me.

"When I'm miserable?" he asks.

Ouch, there's the pain. That's the horror. I make him unhappy. Now that he's said it, it feels undeniable.

"Of course not," I whisper. "Go be happy."

I force myself to choose to let him go then.

"Nina, that's it? Just like that?"

"I tried," I say, "I'll fight with all I have, but I can't fight with what you've got."

I hug him as tightly as I ever have before, and then I open the car door. I get out and start walking down the street to clear my head. The fact that he didn't grab and hold onto me hurts worse than all the pain of my childhood. I have to keep going, though; that's what I tell myself. I just have to keep going. Hope is the pesky thing that tries to keep me company again.

Chapter 39 ~ How Bad Life Gets Better

I think I'd like to live inside a Nancy Meyers movie for a while. In her films, beautiful, perfectly chosen surroundings envelope the characters at just the right time. Everything feels heightened and somewhat better than what the real world delivers. Relationships seem predestined. Although you can't tell who's going to end up with who, it all makes perfect sense in the end, but I know nothing will make sense if I don't get back together with Lens. I know I need to lose sight of my pain for a while.

Sometimes I think of all the people that I could have helped and didn't. I think of people I knew who showed their neediness by what they did and how they spoke. Had I just ignored people in pain? I consider the homeless people I passed without stopping to acknowledge them. I'd been broke, but I could have at least stopped to say hi. Maybe my pain is so deep because I haven't done enough.

I am staying at a hotel room for the night. I just needed to get away or at least feel like I was getting away. I turn on the television and try to relax. I cannot believe that I've lost the love of my life, and the world seems to be all mixed up.

"If you save a life today, you may save it for the long run," the blurry man on the news announces.

Talking heads are discussing the topic I've probably considered the most: suicide. I yawn, stretch, and think of the lyric that Dolly Parton sings about trying to come to life.

I think: *Oh, Dolly, if only I could feel truly alive.*

On television, the panel discussion takes a strange turn when some journalist starts conflating the debate on suicide with one about the right to die. Hearing people talk about suicide makes me angry. It seems so specific and unique to each person who feels tempted by its false solutions. I think about all the things I need to do in the world for others, and I try to lull myself to sleep without letting my mind wander to the dark places it longs to explore.

Long Saturdays spent curled around Leonard seem like many lifetimes ago. Sometimes now I catch myself just staring and thinking a little too deeply, as though I'm in a trance. I think of long ago days with Lens by my side, and I remember the overwhelming joy I'd always feel in his presence. I miss looking into his eyes, tasting his skin, smelling his neck, listening to his familiar voice, and touching his entire body. Selfishly, I miss the way being loved by him made me feel.

I catch myself in one of those Lens trances as I nod off the sleep. I am feeling very tired, like I just need to rest for a while.

Chapter 40 ~ Cousins

I take a deep breath as I feel a jolt. I open my eyes, and I look at the movie screen. Ted Danson and Isabella Rossellini are on a motorcycle; they ride blissfully through the countryside. *Cousins*! I remember this movie, but I saw it as a kid. It had to be made in the 1980's. Oh, gosh, I feel my body and look to my left.

Davey! There's my Davey. I'm back in time once again? I know I didn't die this time. In fact, I'm sure I didn't. That's not it. This isn't hell unless it's something like the third rung of it or maybe a sort of perpetual purgatory.

Whatever is going on, I'm overjoyed to be here once again with Davey. I won't let him go. I can't help reaching over and giving him a huge hug. This makes him uncomfortable.

"Hey, cut it out!" he says, "Go get me some more popcorn, will you?"

Davey hands me $20. I am confused. It's kind of rude to shoo me away in the middle of a movie, but I know that he's moody sometimes. I am just so thrilled to see him. I hand the money back to him. Oh my goodness, how did this happen again? I want to scream right in the theater. How am I going to handle this all over again? Oh, wow, but there's Davey.

"Not now. I'm tired," I say. "Get your own popcorn."

I can tell that he is a bit confused. I know my former child self was such a push-over, but I'm not feeling that right now. I don't know exactly what I'm feeling, but I am pretty self-protective all of the sudden.

It's too painful to look at Davey. He represents the hope of the past, present, and future. I know that I will try to save him again, but I feel defeated before the struggle begins. Being caught in the body of a child feels freeing for a moment, just like it did the first time around.

It's also such a shock to my whole self that I cannot even let the reality of it all sink in at first. It's all a bit too much to bear. There's so much going on inside.

I look at the movie, and I could have sworn that I just saw this one videotape as a kid, not at the movies. How could I go back to something that never happened?

"Will you remind me? What's today's date?" I whisper.

"Nice try. You know it's my birthday, and I happened to know that you already put my birthday present on the living room table. It's signed in that overly neat handwriting of yours and everything."

"Hey, you snooped!" I exclaim in mock outrage.

"That I did, little one," he says jokingly.

The third strike? Could this really be happening again? I realize now how silly it was to think that this couldn't happen again. This weird spiral. I wonder, though, is this really the third time? Was my original life some spiral of this that I was not even aware of? Perhaps, at some point, one forgets, and it's only on some journeys that we remember? Do people who believe in reincarnation get the whole thing completely misunderstood, never realizing that we are forever tied to our specific lives and true selves?

No matter how many times I have passed through this life now, I have only ever ended up as Nina. I only remember three. This is my third. Yet I no longer trust this as simply a new phenomenon. I am looking at the world and trying to spot any differences, and suddenly I feel foolish for not paying closer attention to the world around me during my second go at this. If I had, maybe I could make smart investments now and maybe even figure out how to create a happy sort of life for myself.

I find myself closing my eyes and saying a prayer. I really need to find out if this is maybe God's plan. I remember how much faith I had and how I long to get that back. I remember the indescribable feeling I'd get in my heart when I accepted Jesus, and I wish that the little girl I'd been had never known the shock of losing faith in everything.

Chapter 41 ~ Dust

The second funeral of Davey Gregory Newman was unbearable. I couldn't believe that I lost him again. What's even worse is that I thought we were out of the woods. I honestly believed that things would be different. This time around was worse, though. Maybe because I knew it was inevitable, it was hard for me to enjoy what little time I had with him. Now he's gone, and I don't know how I am going to go on with my life.

My mother's funeral is even worse, and I don't attend my father's funeral. I hope that nobody came to it. He doesn't deserve that. I think he must be such an awful person to be capable of doing the unthinkable so many times now. I feel a pure hatred for him.

I used to be comforted by the fact that everybody thinks of themselves as good people. This morning, though, that thought is terrifying. Imagine all the assholes thinking that they're okay? Justifying what they've done. I can't figure out how people are mean to waitresses, and I have hundreds of memories of strangers treating me like a subpar human because I was serving them for the evening. Once people start justifying treating others badly based on their temporary position in life, anything can follow.

Chapter 42 ~ By the Bell

All the people I meet along the way seem to want to tell me that life must go on. Moving on is too difficult. However, if I was ever actually going to off myself, surely I would have done so by now. The depression I fought so hard against for so long threatens to return, but I am battling it like a champ. I start therapy, although I worry it won't help because I can never tell the psychologist about my echoing problem.

Today I'm starting school again. I am scared and a little unsure of myself. I decide to live for myself, though, and that means learning as much as I can for now. Not a lot of people will take me very seriously until I at least look grown-up.

I smile with such a sense of relief when I see Penny in the cafeteria. Ah, I've missed her so much. Wait, we're not friends yet. A wave of sadness pushes down on me when I realize that I can't be completely open with her like the old days. Aside from the time travel conundrum, I used to tell her every little thought that was on my mind.

Now, I can't tell her how close we once were any more than I can discuss the main things that I'm going through because she could never understand. I wouldn't in her position. Nobody could. I scarcely manage to wrap my head around it most mornings.

I have to at least try to connect with her again, though. I'm sure of my love for her. So I take an empty seat beside her.

"Hi, Penny," I say.

Oh, please let us be friends. It seems preposterous to want to befriend such a kid again now that she doesn't know me. I need to talk to someone, though, even if it's artificial and not real.

Penny nods at me politely, then she opens her book and tries to appear busy. I could swear that she looks down as if she's embarrassed to be seen with me.

"You don't mind if I sit here, do you?" I dare to ask.

"Uh, I kinda do. I was waiting for some other kids," she says with an apologetic frown.

"No problem," I lie.

It's a big problem. I get up quickly and rush out of the cafeteria. I find an empty bathroom stall where I cry as silently as possible. I am older than some of the teachers here, and I shouldn't care about the friendship of this kid. However, I love unconditionally, and it was such a relief to fit in before, to have a friend like her. I'd always wanted so badly to be friends my first try at life. I had shown myself that I could do it. Yet here I am, failing again. I have nobody here. There's no way that I'm making it through school this time.

I pull myself together and decide to hide in the library for the rest of the day. Being around books manages to cheer me up at least a little bit.

"Are you lost, sweetheart?"

I turn around and see the librarian who was so kind to me in high school. Oh, thank goodness! Here's an adult I can talk to! She's a nice one, too. Whew, oh, I resist the urge to throw my arms around her in an embrace, yet she can sense my relief and gives me a big smile.

"I...I'm trying to find a good book...by a writer I'd love."

"What's your name?" she asks.

"Nina...um, Nina Newman."

"I'm Sharon. Most people around here call me Mrs. Trudy, but why don't you use Sharie?"

I smile. She is trying to make me feel special maybe. I can't imagine that she actually likes me. Nobody seems to be able to stand being near me. She pulls a couple of books off the shelf, looks them over, and hands them to me.

"Lucy Maud Montgomery?"

"You've read her before, haven't you?" she smiles.

"I read the Emily books. I loved them. I saw the Anne movie with Megan Follows."

"You know, that's the best book adaptation I've ever seen. Still, you should read the books. They're a different experience…Will they do?"

"Okay," I agree.

Sharie starts to walk back to her desk and motions for me to come along with her. I look at her with so much hope in my heart. Oh, can we be best friends? I wish that I could tell her what I'm going through, but even someone as sympathetic as she seems to be could never believe what I was experiencing. It was hard enough for me to accept it as the truth.

"You come here on your lunch every day? Don't you get hungry?" she asks.

"I'm fine," I lie.

She nods her head as if recognizing my lie with silent acceptance.

"Well, promise you'll let me know what you think of the first book?"

I nod my head, then finally answer, "I promise."

Chapter 43 ~ Wishing Star

I go to my guitar. Thank goodness it's in tune! I awkwardly attack the keys, getting out all my anger and frustration on the strong strings, and the music starts to soothe me. I try to pick out "Wildest Dreams," my favorite song from Taylor Swift's *1989*. That's one of the albums that I miss the most from my old life and original time in this world.

Is this really the same world even? I don't know. I forget these thoughts as I recreate the music that Taylor has not yet created in this timeline. Ten years younger than me, I wonder what little Taylor is doing in the world now. I guess she doesn't yet know how to play the guitar.

I drop back onto the bed and continue to play. The song soothes me. It is such a badass declaration of love without expectations. She knows the pain of a breakup and braces herself for that, but she loves anyway. For a second, though, maybe she won't let herself get emotionally invested. Of course she probably never felt like that for more than a few moments, but those minutes of not caring can be powerful. I want to not care so much.

In some ways, I feel like a teenager. I don't act my actual age. In other ways, I feel a distinct hopelessness that's creeping up despite the coping skills that I should have developed by my true age. No matter how old I am, or how I look, I know that I will never totally feel like an adult. I mostly feel like a little kid who will never grow up.

Chapter 44 ~ On With the Show

Sometimes I get sad before bad things happen. If I suspect that they might occur or probably will, the doom and gloom pervades my every thought long before it should. I work through it, and everything's okay. All is even well. Knowing that sadness is only temporary is probably the best part about growing older.

When I wake up in the morning, I am not ready to exist within a new day. I cannot even manage to crawl through the day, so I go back to sleep, hoping that I'll be able to skip and jump through life when nightfall hits. Nighttime has always been the time when my spirit wakes up and feels comfortable enough to simply be.

When I graduated high school, Mrs. Trudy gave me a box set of *Anne of Green Gables*, and I take it with me everywhere I go. I don't care how much weight it adds to my luggage. I love them.

In my first life, I remember reading about how Lucy Maud Montgomery chose to end her life, and my heart breaks in empathy for her. I ache at the thought of her in that much pain. She brought so much beauty to the world, and I wished I could choose when to travel back in time. I'd like to go back and hang out with her. I know I probably couldn't save her any more than I could save my family, but I'll be damned if I wouldn't try.

I am not sure how to deal with this life, but I stumble through it. I feel the loss of my family and Penny. Things seem to be turning out worse this time. I lost my family, and I feel their loss dragging me to even greater depths of despair. I lost Penny before I even was able to have her as my friend in this lifetime.

I also have a hard time figuring out how to deal with the loss of Lens. I realize that maybe, if we had another chance, we could try to be together forever or at least for more than half a decade. I need more time with him. With all the expanse of space and the span of time, I need to be with Lens at least once more.

I miss Penny too much to go to Paris without her, but I take my chance on a talk that Lens is doing at a conference in Fairhope, Alabama. I have waited far longer than I wanted to wait. I tried once again to change things in 2001, and I couldn't. Now it is the year 2003.

Chapter 45 ~ Pretty Man

Going to a conference just to see Lens feels weird, and I am not so sure that things will even click this time. Perhaps he won't look at me. Maybe I'll be unable to speak with him. I might repulse him. Taking such a huge risk feels a bit like I'm losing what's left of my peace of mind.

As I gather my courage, though, I look at the exterior of the hotel that holds the conference room. It's a beautiful autumn day, and wildflowers of many colors seem to be in bloom everywhere I look. I am always shocked by the beauty of this town when I return to it after any time away at all. It's like I lose sight of how a place could be so lovely until I'm right in the midst of it.

Are you happy? Do you have moments of pure joy every day? Are you adored and treasured in the way that you should be?

Those are the questions that I have for Leonard Daley, artist extraordinaire. I rush into the conference room. It's packed. He is a local hero, and I smile to think about how much joy he has given to everyone in the room. How cool is that? I want to congratulate him, but he doesn't know me. That's the most painful part of it.

Looking back, I remember special things I knew about Lens from the start. He's handsome and also humble. He treats everyone that crosses his path with instant respect and kindness. His eyes are radiant when he finds humor or joy in a situation. He has a beautiful voice and talks with a sort of gentleness that I've found to be quite rare in any human being. He also is interesting in a way that leaves me both satisfied as well as always wanting to know more.

After his talk and presentation, everyone crowds around Leonard. I don't want to be just another fan in the group of many, so I wait in my chair and write in my diary. I start to feel just a little sorry for myself when finally the crowd starts to file out. I walk slowly up to him, and I say hi in a barely audible squeak.

At that exact moment, my stomach growls, and my eyes close tight in embarrassment. I know he heard me, but I'm just going to pretend that it didn't happen. Thankfully, he goes along with that plan.

"Hi, thanks for coming out. Did you enjoy the presentation?" he asks.

"Yes, so very much," I say, then find myself staring into his eyes.

"It makes me feel great to hear that."

"*Autumn Joy*. It changed my life. I...still spend time just getting lost in it," I manage to say.

"Wow, that's wonderful," he says graciously.

What I really want to say in reply is: *You're wonderful.*

Instead, I mutter something meaningless, and I am thrilled when he still invites me to go for a walk.

~

It only takes a couple of weeks for Lens and I to once again fall in love. I have no complaints, and I cannot hold anything back. I just am all about spending time with him, and he seems more excited than ever to see me.

This evening he wears all black. He has a faux silk black shirt tucked into dress pants, with black loafers over black shoes. Yet the colorful, dressy jacket that he's wearing livens up the whole look. It's pastel and subtle, yet the vibrant colors are undeniable. I don't remember him dressing like that in the magical other time that we shared.

Maybe he did, and I just now am more aware of fashion and maybe even more aware of the man he is.

I chose an emerald green dress with a tapered waist. Its medium-length skirt flares out as I twirl in front of the mirror. I just can't resist. I'm feeling too joyful, yet I hear his laugh and hesitate. I invited Leonard to get dressed at my place, but I didn't know he was watching me twirl.

"Please don't stop."

I laugh this time but continue twirling.

"We're going to have fun tonight," I promise him and myself.

"Yeah. I think we will," he agrees.

As I stop twirling and look in his direction, I see a hint of some kind of mischief in his eyes. It's hard to stay on top of what he has up his sleeves or on his mind. It occurs to me that he is the prettiest thing I've ever seen.

~

Lens takes my hand as we stroll through the charming, historical downtown area of Fairhope. After a few moments, he reconsiders and wraps his right arm around my shoulders, and this is everything I ever wanted. I close my eyes and savor every second as I place my head against his chest while we walk. If this is all I get, if this moment is it, it's so much more than enough.

We walk over a small bridge in the park. It's October, and the leaves are wildly dancing in the wind. I feel like joining them. I have to hold myself back from skipping barefoot through the grass and shouting out to the world about how absolutely ecstatic I am.

I love that he and I don't have to say a thing, because words would fail to express what we are to each other, or at least I know that's true for how I feel. Maybe he is just considering what he wants for dinner, but my focus is on us.

As if joking with the thoughts going on in my own head, he says, "I made reservations at this new place I think you'll like."

"For tonight?"

"Yeah. You said you were free and up for a surprise. Would you rather pick the place?"

"No, I like surprises," I say coyly. "I just thought maybe you were playing it by ear yourself."

We go back to the simple, comfortable silence we had before. He holds my hand, and we just walk for a long time. I forget what time it is until the sun starts to set. It's then that I speak again.

"Wait, what time is your reservation?"

"Turn around," he says.

I turn around, and I see an elaborate dinner table set in the middle of an otherwise empty, ornate restaurant. The décor is comprised of red and gold fabrics that display intricate, beautiful designs. The entire restaurant is lit by dozens of candles, and the soft light shows a beautiful atmosphere.

"What is this?" I ask excitedly as he holds the door open for me.

I walk inside as I grab his hand. I marvel at the beauty of this place.

"I thought we'd enjoy some privacy tonight," he says softly.

A host comes up with a smile, taking our jackets and leading us to the table. Lens orders champagne with our appetizers, which strikes me as a rather strong effort. Nothing is too much with him, though. It's all sweet and perfect.

I look down for a moment, observing the beautiful place setting before me. When I look up, I am surprised to see that Lens is no longer in his chair. He has moved to my side. He gets on one knee, and I gasp as I hear what he has to say.

"Will you marry me?"

I have to kiss him before I can reply that, of course, I will marry him. I finally even get around to directly saying, "Yes!"

Chapter 46 ~ Forever

I walk up the aisle. As I do so, I cannot take my eyes off Lens. He is wearing a tuxedo that looks a bit unconventional because of the colorful shirt he wears with it. I just want to stare, so I do. Nobody seems to mind.

I finally have the beautiful white dress that I always imagined. The portrait-perfect, sweetheart neckline elongates my short neck, the barely-there, white sheer sleeves rest on my shoulders. The fitted bodice of the dress flares out into a large, flowery princess skirt.

I think back to *Autumn Joy* and the magical wedding that the painting depicted. I wonder what inspired that piece, but I've never had the courage to ask. I guess I am afraid of being disappointed, but somehow I don't think he could manage to truly disappoint me in any real way.

I feel happier than even the couple in that wondrous painting must have been. As I continue my walk down the aisle, instead of marching for a few steps, I choose to skip. Some of our guests laugh, but it's not at me. I know it's about seeing someone so very happy, or maybe they're recognizing the same joy in themselves. I don't know, but I cannot assume anything but the best in everyone today.

I arrive at the altar, and Lens and I immediately hold one another. When we manage to come apart just a bit to turn to the preacher, Lens puts his left arm around me and his hand on my back. Its V-shaped, open back allows me to feel the heat of his hand directly against my skin, and I feel like I may faint from how intensely pleasurable that simple touch is.

"I now declare you husband and wife!" the preacher declares after we repeat the sweet and simple traditional vows.

The enthusiasm of the preacher is especially endearing, and I have to stop myself from cracking up with happiness as I hear a few friends laughing again. As I walk back down the aisle with his hand in mine, my three-foot-long, chapel train swishes a bit behind me, and I know it's the only part of my past that I can bear to take with me.

I get this feeling like everything's going to be alright. We are setting each other free with this marriage. It's going to be the dawn of something special.

Chapter 47 ~ Dreams Come True

I'm ready for the wedding night. I smile widely as we rush into the honeymoon suite at the most beautiful, elegant hotel in town. It's so close to the water that I hear waves crashing onto the beach when I walk near the window.

Now to seduce my husband! I try to turn around in a sexy way, but I almost fall down instead. Trying to save myself and prove my dancer's grace, I somehow stick out my arms and regain my balance.

"There's something I have to tell you," I say.

"Oh, yeah?" he asks with concern wrapped around his tone.

"You need me right now," I say in as sultry a way as I can manage.

I was going to try to open up to him about my situation, but my lust takes over my thoughts. Fear may be a factor, too. I can't mess this up again.

"What did you just say to me?"

"You heard me," I grin. "You do need me. Make love to me!"

I demand it. I find myself almost yelling. Gah, that's not going to turn him on. I am so burning with desire that making sexual demands is all I can fathom doing in the moment.

"I think that can be arranged," he replies, although he cannot keep from slathering his amusement all over the words he speaks.

I climb on top of him, draping my legs over his handsome hips. I kiss him deeply and passionately. The laugh in his heart escapes as I kiss him. He marvels at my mad desire. He grinds his body against mine, and I feel more alive than I've ever felt before.

As I fall onto the bed after we climax together, I look over at Lens. He is looking at me with satisfaction and a bit of curiosity in his eyes. He puts his left hand under his left cheek and pulls himself partly up with his elbow. He reaches out to touch me with his right hand.

"You're a lot of fun," he says as he caresses me.

I smile because I want to be fun. I intend to create good times for the two of us as often as possible. The more time I get, the stronger my desire gets to not waste a single moment.

Chapter 48 ~ Changing of the Guard

I sit in the kitchen, resting my head in my hands. Where we're living is so perfectly suited for Leonard's temperament. I can see every color of the rainbow from where I sit as well as blacks and browns.

I notice something. There's a painting that I never saw before. Had he only painted it this time? That didn't seem likely with how our other lives had gone.

"Lens," I say when I notice him in the doorway.

It only takes me a few seconds before I meet him in the doorway and have my arms around him.

"Good morning," he says sweetly.

"I have a question. When did you paint this?"

"Oh, last night. You fell asleep right after...I got restless, so I got up to paint a while."

"Wow."

"You really like it?"

"Yeah, that color! It reminds me of...my favorites when I was younger."

"It's yours then," he says as he places it in my hands.

"Wow."

That seems to be my word of the day, and I look at him in disbelief. This is the type of painting that belongs in museums and exquisite displays for all the world to see. It's not simply a painting for my enjoyment. I decide against denying the gift, though. I accept it with a kiss and my sincerest gratitude. It's an extraordinary thing.

He grabs me in his arms then, and he whispers, "If I could take away those things that you make you cry and scream at night, I would. You were having nightmares. When I heard you, I climbed into bed and held you until you fell asleep. Do you remember what you were dreaming?"

I nod my head no, and I feel guilty. Actually, I suspect that perhaps I was dreaming about the time when I lost him in my other lifetime. I wish I could share that with him so we could be even more certain that it won't happen again.

~

I suddenly realize that it's more than the wondrous new paintings from Leonard that seems new in this lifetime. So much is different. I start to worry that perhaps so much is going on that I just don't know how to handle.

My nightmares keep coming back. This time I wake up screaming out loud, and I remember my dream. I feel instantly embarrassed when I see that Lens is now awake, too.

"Nina," he says tenderly, "Tell me. What is it that's haunting you?"

"I dreamed of the past. I was stuck there, and I was being mocked at home and at school. Then time kept descending, and I went back further, and I was being beaten by my dad…and so was Lily."

I choke on my words, and I can talk no longer. Tears continue to flow, and I think of Lily, my dog who I loved so dearly before my dad cruelly killed her. I can't think of Lily without completely losing it, and Lens just lets me cry it out. He kisses my face gently, and gives me tissues as I need them.

"You're safe now," he whispers to remind me, "They can't get you now. If I had it my way, you know what I'd do. I would go back in time and rescue you. I'd do whatever it took, risk everything. I just want to make the hurt go away. What can I do to make you hurt just a little less?"

"Hold me," I cry, and he immediately does just that. He wraps both his arms around me tenderly. He knows how to hold me just tight enough so that I feel completely protected. I can't help but think of Lily, and how I wished that I could have saved her.

Chapter 49 ~ Thinking Out Loud

I hear "You and I" by Eddie Rabbit and Crystal Gayle play on the evergreen radio station, and I don't want to stop listening. I especially like the part about building the dreams they treasure. What I find most special about it, though, is that Lens and I still consider it our song in this lifetime, too.

I find myself getting lost in a fantasy that perhaps Eddie's a time traveler, too, then I dismiss the idea. Of course not. I couldn't hear the song in three lifetimes. Someone who echoed wouldn't do the same art again. I don't think so anyway. That is, unless they were absolutely convinced of the power of their art to do a great deal of good in the world. Maybe people further along their echoing journeys know far more than I do. Maybe they have it all figured out.

I set out sheets of paper all over the coffee table in the living room. I am trying to choose the best charities in this world that I should be supporting. Not much has changed in this timeline that I can see, but I feel compelled to double check. I look up and see Lens coming into the room. He looks somewhat off. I wonder what's on his mind.

"You're not going to save the world today?" he jokes.

"Don't make fun of my work."

"I'm not. I was..."

"I know what you were doing: making fun," I reply as if to make a joke of the whole thing, but it still smarts. If only he knew how much I really am trying to save the world.

"If you're done with that, can we take this upstairs?"

Ah, so now he finally gets right down to it. I see what he was trying to accomplish, and I admit that it thrills me. I'm every bit as eager to make love as he is, so it doesn't take us long to get all tangled up together. These are the days I dreamed of, ones where I get lost in love, and nothing else matters at all.

Another dawn brings a new day, yet my mind is on the time I spent with Lens in bed yesterday. We had the afternoon together, and we were at it again before we both drifted off to an exhausted sleep. I feel marvelously well-rested, but I feel sad when I look over to see that he's already out of bed. I hear the shower going. I had hoped to wake him up myself.

Chapter 50 ~ Got a Secret

I don't want to deal with anything too heavy today. I hope to set the tone by just grabbing a protein bar for breakfast. I read recently how they have as many calories as a candy bar, so it's all the same if you just grab the obvious indulgence. However, I feel better with the health fad label in front of me as I chew.

Lens walks into the kitchen and turns on the coffeemaker. I think it's odd that he's drinking more coffee than hot chocolate lately. Hot chocolate has always been his drink of choice as long as it has extra sugar and cinnamon. I notice that he hasn't told me why he's switching drinks. Shutting me out over something so small worries me. I want to be perfectly close to him.

I try to avoid all forms of hypocrisy in my life whenever and however possible. I think contradictions have a tendency to creep up into all of our lives, but whether we remain oblivious to them is usually a choice. I cannot promise openness and honesty while harboring the secrets of my strange journey through time.

I'm in the world. No, I'm of it. Even as I feel separate from other human beings, as though I'm a whole other entity, I am part of the moving, ever-changing, and most magnificent world. As deeply entrenched as I am in it, though, I am seeking something grander, looking towards the peaks of the mountains. I wonder how much higher they could go, what our view could be from higher peaks, what the world has to tell us that we don't know how to comprehend.

I blink as I try to bring my mind back to the present moment. I am embarrassed to see Lens staring at me as he sips some coffee.

"What?" I ask, feeling suddenly shy and like I want to hide under the kitchen sink.

"Where did you go just now? What is going on with you? Why do the nightmares keep getting worse, and you're becoming so distant?"

"I'm not...I'm...How about I tell you a dream that I had once, and I want you to listen to it all. Try not to judge me or think for a second that I think the dream was real. But will you just listen and try to understand what it was like for me to be within the dream?"

I look into his eyes. I'm asking him a question, but I am really demanding so much more than an answer. What I need is for him to understand what I've been through, even if it's just for a moment.

"Talk to me, honey," he says sweetly. "Tell me about the dream. I want to hear all about it."

A feeling of total relief washes over me. For the moment, I feel free from carrying this overwhelming burden all by myself. However, when I open my mouth to speak, I realize that I cannot tell him about what's really going on.

"I'm sorry. I...I thought I could, but I can't tell you."

"I'm thinking about leaving," I hear Lens say, but I refuse to listen.

"What?" I ask, daring him to repeat it.

"I started thinking about it last night."

"While we were fucking?"

"No. After..."

"I was that bad?"

"Stop it."

"Stop what?" I challenge.

"Sweetheart, I can't. I wish I could. I can't deal..."

"Deal with what?"

"You are hiding something from me. You've basically admitted it. It has to be an affair. If not that, some unfathomable betrayal, or maybe something worse…"

"What could be worse?"

I look up and see tears in his eyes, and his raw pain makes me ache.

"I could end up locked up if I tell."

"In prison?" he asks as I notice a bit of fear creeping into his eyes.

"No. Gah, I wish I had earned some kind of trust from you, some sort of…something that lets you know that I could never hurt anyone. It's not like that," I whisper. "I'm afraid of being committed to a mental hospital or something."

"Just tell me or…"

"You're giving me an ultimatum?"

"It's not like that," he says with a sigh.

I look down to stop the tears that are welling in my eyes. Usually he's able to more freely express his emotions than I am, but I can't fathom life without him. We can't be separated in this world. I still tell myself that we would never have parted in the other life for very long, that we would have gotten back together.

"I'll tell you. When I tell you, though, you may want to leave me anyway. You'll never look at me the same way again. I know that for sure."

Just like that, I break down. I drop into the chair simply because I can't stand up. I drop my head to the table as sobs wrack my body, and I feel his gentle hands massaging my shoulders. Before I can say anything, I'm in his arms, and he is carrying me out of the kitchen.

"What are you doing?" I say as I do my level best to stop crying.

He doesn't respond, but he brings me into the bedroom. As he delicately puts me on the bed, his lips find mine, and I find it difficult to continue sobbing through his kisses. I feel like I can't breathe because I'm so overwhelmed with every possible great and awful emotion. Finally, I force myself to pull away from him when all I want to do is get closer to his body.

"Wait. What? What are you doing?" I manage to say as I gasp for breath.

"I was trying to comfort you, to tell you how much I still love you," he says meekly.

"I'm supposed to be comforted by passion when you just told me you're willing to walk right out the door?"

"Nothing makes any sense."

"You weren't really going to leave?" I ask.

"I don't know. No. Look, just tell me, okay? It's torture not knowing. Whatever it is, I'll still love you."

This feels like an ongoing nightmare, but, for the first time in our shared lives, I don't believe him. He doesn't understand.

"I've heard the way you talk about people who are superstitious. You scoff at concepts like the afterlife and sacred…"

"Is that what this is about? Are you secretly in some kind of cult or something?" he interrupts me to ask his hopeful questions.

I look up, and Lens is looking at me with the sweetest sort of relief and hope. He is desperately trying to believe that I've made this secret into a much bigger thing that it is. I think maybe he wants to believe I was in some kind of sick cult and had a change of heart, but now everything's alright.

"It…I guess it could be explained that way, but only as a sort of metaphor."

"Oh," he sighs.

"Oh. Yeah. The thing is. Okay. Here goes. I went to sleep one day as a suicidal 37-year-old, in a world better than the one we have now, but one that I couldn't…handle. I woke up in fourth grade. I met you. We fell in love. I never told you that I had a secret. Yet, I died. Or so it seemed. Before I was 37. I was only 22 that time. I didn't see it coming.

I wasn't suicidal. I woke in fourth grade again. Further back. Another chance, maybe. That's what I hoped. Only, it didn't really happen that way. I found you. Again. I had to. And I lost you…and now, to have you again…"

I dare to look up at him for the first time since I started my story, and I am not sure how to read his eyes. Is he giving me a poker face? Hiding his true contempt or disbelief? He seems an odd sort of shocked.

"Well?" I ask, eager for a response of some kind.

"You're telling me that…you traveled through time…against your will. That's your secret?"

"Yes."

"Really? You're going to make up a lie that crazy? Rather than just tell me the truth?"

"Lens. That *is* the truth."

I look into his eyes, and I know in that instant that he can never believe me. If I were standing here in his position, I doubt I would believe me. How could anyone believe a story like that?

"I love you," he says. "I still love you. If you are so afraid of me that you can't tell me the truth, then I've failed you. It's my fault. I shouldn't have threatened to leave. Do you…want me to go?"

"No!" I say so eagerly that we both laugh.

"I'll never leave you," he promises.

I run over to him and give him an embrace that's tighter than I've ever given anyone.

Chapter 51 ~ Trust

I wake up and feel somehow as though I'm on camera. Someone's watching me. I'm sure of it. It's just a strange feeling that is validated when I look up to see Lens watching me from the doorway.

"What are you doing?" I ask with a laugh.

"I believe you," he says.

Well, that wakes me up. I hop out of bed and run to the doorway. I fling my arms around him and let out all the emotions I've been keeping inside.

"What changed your mind?"

"You. Thinking about it all. How is it that we so easily go together?"

"Oh, do we have a lot to catch up on," I squeal.

The home phone rings, and I want to tell Lens to ignore it. I want to let him do whatever he wants to do, though. So I watch him as he picks up the phone and casually puts it to his ear. He seems surprised as he turns to me.

"It's for you."

I got to the phone, feeling a little strange since I never give that phone number to anyone. I prefer the easy control of my cell phone, and I like how I can simply turn it off whenever I need to recharge myself for more social time.

"Who's this?" I ask in the friendliest way possible.

"I saw you at Show Biz."

"You were at the bar, and on the plane?" I ask breathlessly.

Lens is looking at me. He's curious, and I fear that he may get suspicious all over again. I still have to know. I need to understand what's happening if I can live in peace with my husband. I make a motion for Lens to give me a moment, and I step outside with the portable phone.

"Why are you contacting me? What do you want? Why have you stayed away for so long?" I say into the phone.

"Meet me outside in two minutes."

"Outside my house?"

"Yes, exactly where you are right now."

I swallow hard as the line goes dead.

Chapter 52 ~ Shock

Life is just too difficult. I have to find a way to end it all. No, I just think I do for this intense moment. I remember that everything passes. I can find a way to go on. The strange man asked me to wait outside, and so I am. I pace quickly. I'm afraid that Lens will come out to check on me before man arrives, and I'm afraid that he won't.

I look up as a dark grey car stops right in front of the walkway. The electronic window comes down on the passenger's side, and I see that the strange man who has haunted my nightmares is behind the steering wheel. He turns to me.

"Get in," the man says.

I look back towards the house. For a horrifying moment, I consider how awful it would be if I never saw Lens again. I have to know what is going on, though. Without letting myself further consider the possibilities, I get into the passenger's side. I laugh at myself when I automatically go to fasten my seatbelt, as if that could keep me safe.

"So?" I say.

The car ignition was never turned off, and he speeds away. I look back at my house one last time, and I see Lens standing in the doorway watching me in the car. I wave weakly, and I see tears welling in his eyes. What he must think of me! Does he think I'm just leaving without telling him? I guess that's what I am doing.

"I have to tell you something," the stranger says.

I always hate when anyone does that. It's the worst when people tell you that they want to talk to you about something gravely serious, then expect you to wait for a long time. That makes minutes feel like days and seconds like hours.

"No shit," I exclaim, then regret my own harshness.

"I sense a certain level of resentment…"

"If you have to tell me something, just say it," I sigh, losing my patience.

"I'm the reason that you're going through all this," he confesses.

"Why I am going through the torment of driving with a stranger to who knows where?"

"No, Nina. Listen to me. I'm the reason you're going through all this. I brought you back in time."

"Stop messing with me. I've been…We just met. I've been going through this since…1989. I mean, it's been so many years now since I was thrown into this hell. That's not counting the time before."

"Yeah. It took me a long time to find you this time. Once I did, I was terrified of coming into your life."

"Both times. You took me back both times?"

"Yeah."

"So I…I did kill myself in 2016?"

"No, you were murdered."

'By who?"

"Me."

"What?" I ask.

I begin to get hysterical while a bigger part of me also goes numb. I'm afraid that I am going to go into a state of terror and never recover.

"But I didn't die the second time?"

"No, you didn't."

"So dying has nothing to do with going back in time?"

"No. What sort of novels have you been reading?"

"Oh, believe me, when it comes to time travel, I've read all the fiction and non-fiction. I've seen all the movies, too," I say with a bitter laugh. "I consume anything that pertains to time travel."

"After I killed you, I freaked out. I had been studying so many different theories about time travel for years and years. We'd been working on a secret project. A whole big group of us. We had a private chat board where we shared ideas. I took advantage and tried everything. I couldn't bear to live in a timeline where I'd killed you, and..."

"But I didn't die in the second...echo? People call it echoing?"

"Yeah, that's what some people call levels of time travel. My group...we started that."

I marvel at the pride in his voice. I am so confused. What kind of crazy man is this?

"Your group? Why the hell did you kill me to begin with? I didn't even know you. What are you saying? I need to know the whole story. I was going to kill myself that night, but I couldn't. Not when I saw something that reminded me of why...life is worth living."

"It is. You're right. I shouldn't have come that night. If I hadn't, would you have had a happy rest of your life, do you think?"

"Why did you do it?" I ask, ignoring his question because I have no answer.

"I know your ex," he said finally. "I'm sorry. He was once a part of our group. Not anymore. He told me some things. I should have known they weren't true. When I actually looked at you, I knew that what he said couldn't haven't been true, but it was too late. I'd pulled the trigger at the back of your head. I sat there, and I read the diary you had by your bed. I fell...It was so beautiful. I just wanted to rescue you...So I...I tried, and it worked. It's as clumsy and awful as that."

"So, why not just leave it at that? Yes, you brought me back in time and went back yourself....But...Why do it again?"

"You're happier, aren't you? Isn't this really the life you wanted?"

"Well, yes…I am happy…but…"

I was so caught up in our conversation and overcome with my own fears that I never noticed that we circled back around to my very own neighborhood. I realize that he has stopped in front of my home. I look at the porch and see Lens sitting there. He looks bereft. I am so totally confused. It can't be this simple. It can't be this complicated and weird.

"I wanted to talk to you to say that I'm sorry. I didn't mean to give you such a fright. I've been checking up on you, and usually I don't get caught. Those few times you saw me, those were accidents. You almost never saw me. The time I called you…I was trying to tell you, and I chickened out."

"So what? What now?"

"Go. Be free."

He unlocks the car door. So many questions are still spinning in my head, but I have a strange feeling that this is the only chance I will have to get out of the car and run to Lens. So I do just that before I can even think twice about it. The stranger mutters something about seeing me again, but he closes the car door before I can question him. He speeds off as I realize that I never did get his name.

Lens comes over to me and drapes his arms around me. He rests his head on my shoulder, and I grab his head in my hands.

"Everything's okay," Lens assures me, although he can't possibly know that.

"Everything's okay," I tell him. "It really is."

Chapter 53 ~ Nature, Nurture, and Next Her

I open my eyes. I feel incessant panic as I try to stand up, but I stumble back down. I see sterile walls, tacky plastic tables, and ugly orange chairs. I'm tied to machines. I hear beeping. I look all around. Of course. This must be...I'm in a hospital. How did I get here? I feel my body. Oh, no. My breasts and curves are gone.

I cringe as I try to pull an IV out of my arm. I am not going to stay in bed and remain hooked up to all this equipment. I have to see what's going on. I struggle with the IV, but I'm so weak.

I think: *I'd rather be anywhere but here.*

The hospital machines seem to be beeping at an ever-increasing volume. While they may be literally sending signals to assure the nurses and doctors that my heart's beating at an acceptable rate, they sounded like a countdown to some morbid inevitability.

A nurse with the name tag Sam enters. She's followed by a group of interns and a doctor. I start to get a grip on having gone back in time again. I get angry at the stranger in the car who made me feel that I wouldn't have to go back in time again, and I suddenly feel hopeful about the chance to maybe save Mom and Davey this time around.

"What's today's date?" I ask the doctor. "I gotta get out of here."

"Calm down, Nina. We're very glad to see you're awake. It's Friday, October 13."

"Of what year?" I ask, feeling a growing panic in my chest.

The doctor looks very concerned as she replies, "1989."

"No! What about Mom and Dad…and Davey?" I scream.

Sam looks at the doctor.

"They…Sweetheart, they passed. You've…been in a coma for…"

No, no, no, no, no. It's not fair. This time I didn't even get a chance. Not only did I not have a chance to save Davey, but I also didn't get a chance to save Mom. I couldn't talk about it with anyone. How do you tell someone the truth?

Losing Davey once was an unbearable burden, and so many losses compound on each other over and over again. They make going on a constant struggle. I've always been able to see things through a love-tinted view. It intensifies everything at all times. It gives a push to the hard things to make them easier to take with you and massages wounds even as they happen. As the protection of the love-tinted view is fading with every hateful thought that passes through my worried mind, the world is becoming a scarier place.

I notice that one of the nurses turns on the radio of the boom box that someone left on my side table. "Don't Worry, be Happy" comes on the radio, and I'm thankful that the world hasn't changed enough to prevent this recording. It reminds me of when it came on during a fourth grade field trip. We stopped for pizza at this cheap little buffet cafeteria, and Mrs. Woodworth told me to listen to the lyrics of the song. She knew what an anxiety-ridden little mess I was.

I think that I'll stop pursuing relationships with the people that I knew in my previous lives. As much as I love them dearly, it is so painful to meet them all over again and make them love me yet another time. The pressure is always so great to not let on that I know all their stories and suppress all the things I want to confess to them. And what do I really add to their lives? Of that, I'm not sure.

Why did that man make me feel that things were going to be okay, only to pull the rug out from under me right away. Leonard had accepted me. Even knowing the crazy truth, that time, it was okay with him.

Chapter 54 ~ Never Give Up

There's a moment when I start to wonder if everyone has echoed. I imagined myself speaking directly to God at the end of my life. Asking him for just one more day. I imagined that, had I known exactly how things would turn out, I'd still have asked for the time that I did get with Leonard.

I focus on giving back through learning art, volunteering to help others directly, and finding a way to make a lot of money so I can earn to give. I feel good about establishing a purpose, but I live in fear of losing it all in a second.

Finally, I can't take it any longer. I'm in my twenties in this lifetime, and I'm longing for the joy I once knew for far too brief a time. I make a plan to return to Lens again. I figure out which parks he frequents when he wants to enjoy himself. I hate myself for loving so deeply and trying so hard when we may never be together again. I refuse to give up hope, though.

I see Lens from a distance, and my heart feels like it becomes whole just a moment before it shatters. I pull open the book I'm reading as I lean against a tree, praying no stranger comes along to make small talk, because making a single squeak will surely release the lake of tears I can release at any moment if I so much as think of Lens. My love for him is still thriving.

I look at him once again, then I have to look away. There's this thing just being around him does to me, whether it's over the phone or listening to a voice mail message. I taste the bitterness of the fact that he couldn't possibly feel the same way about me, yet I wander closer to where he is.

Recently I read an article in a fashion magazine that told me about the "perfect" way to get a guy. According to a writer, I'm supposed to get a guy to fall for me by acting all into him, then canceling the date at the last minute. Next, I must get him interested again by lavishing him with affection, then give another mixed message. Who would fall in love that way? If that's the psychological way to manipulate a man into feelings of love, the human race is better off without romance.

I know better, though. The world is enhanced, and maybe mostly worth living, because of love and romance. I am either a hopeless romantic or a hopeful romantic. Either way, I am a romantic and will be as long as I'm alive. Without the manipulation, I have to know if it's possible for him to fall for me again.

I have to be absolutely certain that I tried everything I possibly could to show him that I care. I must know that I never gave up. Not until I had absolutely no chance at all. As long as there was any fraction of a full percent of hope that I could be with him again, I had to try even if it meant risking everything else I had going for me.

I am so lost in the thoughts of my love for Lens that I don't realize that I have actually gotten so close to him that we bump into each other. He looks up from the book he was perusing, and he smiles at me.

"You look about as scared of me as I am you," says Lens. "I mean, as scared as I was before I realized you were standing here. I didn't mean to bump into you. I guess that goes without saying, huh? I got a little too interested in this book."

"What book are you reading?" I ask.

"A novel called *Bid Time Return*," he says. "It's very interesting."

"Do you remember me?" I ask, trying to act casual as I put away my own book.

He smiles politely, and I can feel as though I know what he's thinking. It's almost like I can read his mind. I hope that he cannot read mine. I realize that I'm probably projecting and am likely totally clueless about what he really thinks and feels.

"I wish I could say that I did," he says.

Something about his face changes. He becomes almost embarrassed; I wish that he would truly remember me. He must, or is it misplaced hope again? Hope sometimes makes me feel like I'm just watering a tree so I can hang myself from it.

He stands there looking at me. It almost feels like a game of chicken. I stare back. In fact, looking into his eyes is completely heavenly. He has amazing eyes. Something about the way I look at him either scares him or elates him. Perhaps both.

"Say, um, hey, would you like to have lunch…at my place? I mean, I'm cooking anyway…"

"Well, with an offer like that…" he teases me.

"Pretty please?" I say as I scrunch up my eyes against the sun.

"Sure. Right now?"

"Right now. There's no time like the present," I reply, truly appreciating the meaning of those words.

Lens flashes his radiant smile my way, and I'm reminded of yet another reason why I'm still so desperately in love with this man. Suddenly I realize that I don't have any of the foods he loves at my place, and I don't want to blow this chance with him.

"Actually," I say, "I'm so sorry, but could we make it dinner tonight instead of lunch right now? I just realized that I have to be somewhere in half an hour."

I hate lying to him. I will only do it this once. I refuse to become a liar. The only thing I must conceal is my journey through time, whether it's echoing or something else entirely.

"Okay, I don't mind if I do have dinner with you this evening, Miss, uh…?

"Oh, right. I'm Nina. And you are?"

"My name is Leonard. You can call me Lens."

"Okay, Lens."

Chapter 55 ~ Prepare

I'm a distraction in my own life. I cannot move forward because I keep tripping myself up with the mess of simply being me. I managed to volunteer my time today at a community center as well as prepare the meal that's waiting on the living room table. I'm expecting Leonard any minute.

I notice a weird, small black bug flying around the kitchen. Maybe it was drawn to the smell of the peach cobbler in the oven, but do bugs even have a sense of smell? I try to imagine myself as a bug, but I can't seem to wash the sugary dough completely off my hands after three rinses. My mind wanders from daydreaming about bugs to fevered memories of making love to Lens.

I started to buy the groceries to prepare all of Leonard's favorite foods when I realized that he hasn't had a chance to tell me what they are in this life. Oops. So I put most of the ingredients back, but I kept the peaches, flour, sugar, and spices. I figured I could get away with making a peach cobbler. So what if it's his favorite dessert? Don't many people like peach cobbler? Maybe he'd even see it as a divine sort of signal.

I smile when I think about that. I'd like to think that God is so supportive and resolutely on my side. I want to believe that He'd do things like inspire Leonard to understand that little magic coincidences were signals that he should like the short, silly girl with the shattered self-esteem and wide hips.

I hear a knock on the door, and I get so excited. I have dressed to the nines. I have on a figure-hugging pastel blue dress on. It comes in at my waist and barely has sleeves.

Chapter 56 ~ To Attach

We had the most wonderful dinner where we spoke to one another so easily that it was as though we had never parted. Now he helps me take the dessert dishes to the kitchen when his arm accidentally brushes up against my chest. I smile meekly and move aside.

"How is it possible that you cooked a better version of my favorite food than I've ever had before?"

I wish I could say: *Because you helped me perfect the recipe in another life and time when we were so effortlessly happy together.*

Suddenly I worry that maybe he will like me for all the wrong reasons. Maybe he will fall in love with this dish that he doesn't know was partially his original creation.

If you think too much about something, it's worse than not considering it at all. Just the worry that he won't love me makes me feel empty inside. I feel sort of spiritually sore. Loving someone unconditionally isn't what I thought it would be.

"You know, I've been looking for the right time to say this," he says with a smile. "I'm with someone. Dating someone. I hoped you had invited me over as...a friend?"

"Friend?" I say, "Um, sure."

I want to scream at him: *Friend! You don't even think I've known you for an entire day. How could you accept my dinner invitation as a friend?*

I know I am being unreasonable, though. A simple, shared dinner is not a commitment, and we didn't even establish that this was a date. He's right, and I'm wrong. He wins, and I lose. I am so embarrassed.

"I didn't mean to imply that I thought you were into me anyway," he says.

I think: *Oh, Lens, you're so forever humble and incredibly handsome, but I'm as close as I've ever been to just charging at someone like a ram.*

I wonder what his girlfriend is like. I bet he wants some kind of bad ass chick that just isn't me. As he tries to tell me how I should behave to better attract men, I want to say that he's the only man I care about attracting. No matter how much I love him, though, the conversation absolutely exhausts me.

"Why don't you come to the studio and meet her?"

"Meet your girlfriend?" I ask.

"Yeah, you seem like such a kindred spirit. I bet we'll all get along so well. Have dinner at the studio with us tomorrow night? Hell, maybe we'll become regular dinner buddies."

"Okay," I say, knowing that this is the cruelest thing I've ever done to myself.

Chapter 57 ~ Chocolate-Covered Death

Rejection is so casually uncomfortable and unbearably painful at the same time, but I'm no stranger to it. I wonder if the pain of knowing that Lens is happy with another would hurt more or less if I wasn't so very familiar with cold, hard rejection.

Sometimes I also wonder about the last thoughts that went through my dad's head. Since he offed himself, I can't imagine that they were very lovely, and I doubt very seriously that they had anything to do with me. Occasionally, though, I let myself pretend that he was thinking of me and that he regretted all his cruelty. Maybe, for one second, he wanted to hug me and tell that everything was going to be okay.

I think about the closest I came to truly ending it all myself. It happened in college. I was lucky to even be in school, and I knew it. Yet deep, dark depression can creep up on the lucky ones, too.

I was just a teenager with absolutely no coping skills, and I'd been rejected yet again. I had been very careful all my life to never assume any boy "liked" me. I had been taught in high school that guys found me repulsive, and I was not going to put myself on the line for any further embarrassment.

On my first day of college I met this guy named Mitch. He went out of his way to show me that he actually did like me. At least that's what it seemed like when he'd give me his undivided attention. He followed me around and talked to me on breaks from class. He'd say nice things when this friend of his would say something snide or rude to me.

In retrospect, Mitch was just being polite or, if it was flirting, was just something he did as naturally and easily as breathing. When I tried to give him a cupcake on his birthday, though, he refused to accept it, and he made fun of me in front of the entire class. Everyone laughed at me as though I was Carrie White, who had become my kindred spirit film character. Stephen King always had a way of writing strong female characters that I totally understood.

That moment when Mitch rejected my cupcake was imprinted on my memory in a way that only far worse tragedies should be. It confirmed all my doubts and fears. It verified that I would always be a loser, and no man could ever love me. After all, why would any man love me if my own father couldn't manage to do so?

I knew I was being self-pitying, but I always felt that self-pity serves a very useful purpose in this world. I mean, if you're not getting compassion from those around you, it's comforting to give it to yourself even if it's overly indulgent and crosses the line to becoming a full force pity party.

I know now that lots of people are publicly humiliated, and they don't end their lives. I'm also aware that far worse problems than being unworthy of cupcake acceptance plague other people. In hindsight I can try to lock down exactly what brought me so far down to that hopeless place, but I doubt that those who go through with suicide even fully understand that part of it.

In the moment, the pain became unbearable, as though the rejection was the last straw that contributed to my inability to cope with life. I walked from my New York City dorm down to the Kmart on Astor Place. I looked for a rope. I really needed to just end my life since that's the only way I could imagine a cessation of the pain.

I sobbed as I shopped; I was never one for controlling my emotions very well unless I was in a "numb" period, and this was not one of those safe times. I was desperate. Reminders of things that made me happy seemed to only stab at me as I shopped. I had to keep my mind focused on finding the rope.

Through my teary stupor I managed to ask someone where hardware was. Perhaps the rope would be there! He pointed me in the direction with a look of confused sympathy. I thanked him as best I could.

I found the rope after some searching, and I slowly brought it to the counter. I did not rush, but I also didn't linger very long. It was time to end it. The cashier seemed to look at me with curiosity about my single rope purchase, and tears continued to roll down my face as I realized the implications of my purchase. She didn't hesitate, and I paid her in cash.

I strolled back to my dorm. It was getting late. I wanted to see my friends, but I was really shy. I loved being with friends, but I failed to understand why anybody would want to be friends with me. It was all so nice, but I felt undeserving. I believed that perhaps they all secretly hated me.

I folded the shopping bag over the rope a few times, hoping that it would disguise the contents of the bag if I did happen to run into anybody I knew. Mitch, the guy who had so thoroughly broken the pieces that were left of my already shattered heart, just so happened to be waiting for the elevators at the same time I was. How embarrassing. He didn't say anything to acknowledge my existence.

I smiled a bit. I knew he hated seeing me more than I loved seeing him; in spite of the awkwardness, I had felt a surge of joy in my heart at the sight of him. He had been hope at one point.

I got off at the eleventh floor and strolled to my room. I had my key out so that I could quickly get into my room. It was small with a loft bed. I climbed up to the bed with the rope in my hand. I was so very tired by that point, though, so I tossed the rope back down to the floor. I would deal with that tomorrow.

The next day I skipped class. A friend came over after class, though, and enticed me to go spend the weekend with her family on Long Island. What would be the harm in a two-day delay in my suicide plan? I decided to go with the flow and enjoy one last weekend with a dear friend. I came back to my dorm on Sunday. I made an excuse to leave early because I wanted to go ahead and get this over with.

After paying for the train back that Sunday, I had no more money at all. I had to walk back to my dorm room instead of taking the subway because I couldn't afford the fare.

I was desperate for some chocolate, yet I couldn't even scrape together enough to go buy a candy bar at the convenience store. I called my bank hoping for a spontaneous change in the balance, but there was none.

So, finally I looked at the rope. Kmart was open for another two hours. For the sake of a bit of chocolate, I returned the rope.

As I was handing the rope to the cashier, I thought that perhaps I truly did want to live after all. The cashier gave me a full refund, and I rushed to the candy section to grab my favorite type of candy: peanut butter cups.

I paid for the chocolate and walked straight to the only museum nearby that was still open. I hid among the art, knowing that the museum had an original work by Leonard Daley on display. I knew right where it was, in a prime corner on the second floor. I needed his art to reassure me that life was still worth living, and it did just that as I looked at longingly.

I wonder now if I did the right thing so many years ago. I marvel at my ability to find hope in art and the simple pleasure of chocolate. I suffered in silence. I enjoyed wonderful days of pleasure and joy and wonder, and I've always appreciated life so much. It's hard to explain how one can be thankful for her blessings and also want to commit suicide. If you've been there, though, I'm sure you know what I mean.

Chapter 58 ~ Better Than Me

As I walk into the art studio of Leonard Daley, I am amazed at how I'm able to keep myself together. Unrequited love is one thing, but this is something else entirely. It feels like every rejection I ever faced hitting me all at once when I'm completely weak and vulnerable. I consider myself lucky that I'm even able to repress my tears. I have to keep it together, though, and I plaster a slight smile on my face.

Lens leads the way. He greeted me with a sweet hug at the door, and now he is taking me into his studio to meet his girlfriend. I am meeting the love of the man that I love.

I am distracted somewhat by my impromptu tour. The studio is as eclectic and unique as he is. It's something completely different than what he had when he was with me.

It doesn't take me long to realize that every single wall in the studio is a different color. No two walls in any room are even a similar shade. I see rosewood pink, mint cream green, powder blue, and turquoise walls in the lobby. A single desk, chair, and blank canvas are in the lobby; there's nothing more but open space.

Lens opens the door beside the desk. A staircase is hidden behind the door, and each step is painted a different color, creating a rainbow stairway.

For a moment, I forget why I'm here and delight in the moment. I don't know how long I can be here. Just to be here, though, near him, spending time with him. That's enough for just this second.

I love Lens more deeply than anybody else could ever love him. I'm sure of this fact. I don't care how deeply other girlfriends have loved him. I don't know what he experienced with his exes. I just know that I love him without end. I would treat him like he deserves to be treated.

"Are you okay?" he asks.

Oh, no. I am being so rude by getting lost in thought and ignoring him while he's actually in front of me.

"I'm fine," I manage to reply.

I hate lying to him, but I want to protect him.

I look up to see the ceiling fan twirling and feel like getting up and spinning in circles with it. This seems like a brilliant idea, so I do. I hear Leonard's soft, musical laughter and feel that he's watching me. I don't feel that maybe he thinks I am a little nutty to be twirling around like a giddy schoolgirl. I just know that I am driven on joy and instinct.

"Are you okay?" he asks again, this time with amusement coating his tone of voice.

I want to say: *No way.* However, I nod my head up and down once, offering him an easy way out of asking the question. I have a hunch that he doesn't actually want to hear the answer. I'm messy and full of needs. I won't be okay until he loves me.

I think maybe I just want to stay in a bubble and hide from the world forever. A wave of fear washes over me, and all I want to do is run away. I want to leave him in peace. I want to not dare approach the man that I've wanted for so many years.

A woman in an orange floral skirt and tight-fitted T-shirt walks through a back door. It must be his girlfriend Janet because she walks slowly and confidently to Lens. I'd call it strutting even. She smiles at me with a friendly wave, then she kisses him and whispers in his ear.

"That's the girl?" I hear Janet whisper in his ear.

"Hey," I manage to chirp nervously.

Janet is beautiful with wide eyes and tall legs that she shows off with her short skirt. She looks like she just walked out of a photo shoot for a fashion magazine. Something about her seems so sweet, too. I want to dislike her, but she hasn't given me a single reason to do so.

They seem so sweet together, and Lens takes Janet's hand in his as they walk into the kitchen. This is more painful than I imagined, mainly because it seems like the two of them are perhaps even more perfectly suited for each other than he and I were.

Maybe she makes him happier than I ever did. Maybe in all future existences, if there are any, he should be with her because that time would be spent in a higher state of bliss for him. It's also possible that I'm just projecting my fears and insecurities on a couple who may not even be all that serious about each other.

You know you love someone when you want the other person's happiness no matter how it causes you pain. I'm not talking about masochistic self-sacrifice, but simply the willingness to place someone's needs as a priority and fight for another's happiness regardless of the circumstances because you love the person.

As Leonard comes back into the room with a cocktail for me, I excuse myself to go to the bathroom. As soon as I lock myself into the lovely bathroom that's full of wicker and pink, I realize that Janet has made her mark on their home in a way that I never did. They are comfortable together.

I grab my cell phone and set my alarm to ring in ten minutes. My smartphone alarm makes the same sound as my ringtone, so I have hatched a plan to make my getaway. I may wish Leonard the best, but seeing and hearing about the coupling of these two lovebirds is more than I can handle.

I return to the dining room where Lens and Janet sit at the table. I turn to Lens and simply want to say: *It's your happiness that matters most of all to me.* Come hell or high water, that's the truth of it. If it was a choice, that would be incredibly stupid in a way, but feelings are crazy things that appear whether you choose them or not. They come and go as they please, and they don't give a damn about your timeline or happiness.

I hear Leonard make a self-deprecating joke, and I get annoyed at how hard Janet laughs about it. I wonder if she treats him well. If she did, there's no way that he would be insecure when he's that perfect. Of course that's a silly idea. The most amazing people are the ones that never realize how great they are, right? What could be more appropriate? Humility just makes someone more awesome. Also, who was I kidding? Janet probably dotes on him.

Suddenly, though, Leonard jumps in his chair. He looks as though he's in shock and disoriented. He then stands, pushing his chair to the floor as he grabs the table with his hands.

"Nina! You're here. What's going on?" he asks.

I see terror in his eyes, and I wonder if he's taken some kind of weird drugs. Why wouldn't I be here?

"Are you okay, hon?" asks Janet as she stands.

Janet picks up his chair and slowly guides him back into it.

I know I'm imagining things when I perceive Leonard to stare at her with contempt.

As if on cue, my cell phone alarm goes off, and I grab it. I feign disappointment.

"I'm terribly sorry, but will you excuse me a minute?" I ask.

"Of course," Janet answers.

I think: *Don't talk to me. I've loved him longer than you have.*

Of course I don't say that. I smile and walk to the living room as I talk into my cell phone to the alarm that I am in the process of dismissing.

"Oh, I see. Well, can't you wait? No? Okay. I'll be right there."

I return to the two of them with a frown plastered on my face. I try to make my words sound sincere.

"I'm so sorry, but I have to go. I really hate it. Let's make this up another time, okay?"

We agree to meet again, but I know that I am going to leave Lens in peace as long as he is with Janet. It almost seems too good to be true when Lens whispers in my ear that he needs to see me tomorrow. I find the strength to ignore the request. I hug them both good-bye, and I reach up to give Lens a kiss on the cheek. It's one that says good-bye.

When it all comes down to it, I would choose for him to be happy in whatever way works best for him. However, there's too much hope in me to let myself admit that he will never want me. I can't help but conceive of a possible time in the future, when perhaps he is happier without her. It is the ultimate in selfish thinking, but I'm not fighting my flaws tonight. Sometimes what helps you make it through the night are thoughts of all the wrong things, and maybe that's okay just some of the time.

Chapter 59 ~ Forward Thinking

I tried to move on a lot of times before I actually started going in that direction. I am giving blood again every two months, although sometimes I wonder if the people I help in this lifetime are somehow helped in yet another timeline. I doubt it. I confuse myself easily these days.

I volunteer for several organizations that help human beings and other animals. Effective altruism still strikes me as one of the most important concepts. I study philosophy and work on balancing my desire to create art that helps others and actually doing the direct work I know will save lives. Even if I don't remain on this exact world and time to see how I help them, surely I still do. I go on faith here, and faith is something I'm rediscovering each day.

Perhaps the main thing I learned from my decades-long struggle with suicidal depression is that the bad feelings pass. I discovered that life is not about me. I mean, my life is *my* life. You'd think it would be about me, but it's just not. I want to use my life to help things get better. By staying alive, I can help so many who I may never even meet.

It's the difference between being massaged and being stabbed. That's what an afternoon is like for me now versus how it was while I was afflicted with suicidal depression. I selected those somewhat simplistic metaphors because I now actively choose to take extra special care of myself; I used to actively hurt myself in many ways because of the huge amount of mental anguish I felt. I now find joy in the day. Before it was suffering and agony and wanting the pain to stop so desperately that I simply wanted out of life.

There are different levels of desire, and I can go beyond my limits to overcome what was done to me. There is the most basic level of wanting something, but there is a level above that. There's wanting to want something, then there is wanting to want to want something. I feel that a lot of my power lies in the choices I make about the level I feed.

I still think of Lens. On my darkest days, I wish that I had met him in the small space of time before I learned that I didn't matter and that I would never be good enough, no matter what I did, to truly be in his world. Maybe my very unworthiness, of cupcake acceptance or anything else, is why I am marching through such confusion. On most days, though, I see my worth with how I help others and who I'm becoming.

Chapter 60 ~ Jeans and Polka Dots

It's a beautiful fall morning. Years have passed since I had my heart on the line. I manage to carry on, but I don't invite others into my heart or my life. So I'm both thrilled and scared when I spot Lens as I walk past a café I used to frequent.

Lens sits at a small table outside. I know that he's drinking hot chocolate with cinnamon and extra sugar, and I feel special to know all of his favorite things.

"I love you more than anything," I whisper to him, knowing full well that I'm so far away that he cannot hear me.

It's easier to be honest when you know someone can't hear a word you say. Also, I know he doesn't feel that way. He can't feel that way. He has a bigger life, one of complications that I've never known. If he loves me at all, it certainly isn't more than anything else in the world. That doesn't change my own feelings in any way.

I slowly wander closer to him; I know he might spot me soon. The overcast day and lighting in the café make his hair seem silvery as it blows in the small breeze. His dark eyes are lost in thought. The familiar ache for him rises in the frenzied way it does every time I see him.

Our eyes meet, and Lens holds my eyes in his gaze. I finally give him a slight smile, which he takes as an invitation to grin. I look away, suddenly scared as my pulse races. I can't do this again, so I take off down the walkway at a rapid pace.

I hear him call my name, but I can't stop. Before I realize it, I trip over an uneven spot on the sidewalk. Losing my balance altogether, I fall flat on my ass. I try to catch my breath as the shock of the fall releases the tears I've been repressing. I quickly wipe them away and force myself to appear composed because, from the sound of gentle, approaching footsteps, I know Lens is nearby. When I look up again, I see his smiling eyes.

"Nina, what the hell are you doing? Are you okay?"

He laughs, so I do, too. I nod to signal that I'm okay because I know that my voice will crack, and tears will come again, if I do anything more. I look away so that the pain isn't darting out of my eyes. I suspect that he knows why I'm suddenly so interested in looking at the brick wall of the building to the right, but he mercifully lets the lull in conversation go on without making it worse.

"Positively sure you're okay?" he finally asks.

He reaches down and offers me his hands. As he helps me to my feet, I look at him more closely. Ah, how I want to reach up and kiss him.

"Yeah, I'm absolutely convinced. Just a little weirded out today."

"Oh, yeah? Why's that?"

What do I say? That I am overcome with a desire for him to take me right there in the street? That I've loved him for longer than he's been alive, even if that doesn't make sense, and nobody would ever understand or believe me? That I'm still madly in love?

"Long story," I finally say as he looks at me quizzically.

"Can we sit and chat for a bit maybe?" he asks.

"Yeah," I barely say.

I cling to any way that I can speak casually because that's how I am faking what it takes to talk to him without grabbing him in my arms. We both start walking the few steps back to the café.

"You're going to think this is crazy...and maybe a little terrible...I felt like we almost had something...and...well, you know..."

Something doesn't ring true in what he's saying. I know him. He's holding something back.

"We didn't have long enough," I whisper.

My own words take me by surprise. Up until that moment, I had always told myself that living in the moment made each millisecond enough. That the few fleeting moments in time that I had spent with Leonard were more than I deserved; I told myself that I couldn't dare ask for more. Yet what I want to do in this moment is ask for more.

Instead, I sit down at the café table where he'd been sitting before. He sits down, too, and looks tenderly at me.

"How's Janet?" I ask.

"We broke up a long time ago," he replies as he looks down and takes a sip of his hot chocolate.

"I'm...I'm sorry that I can't say I'm sorry. Part of me wished that she was a bitch and that you would dump her. She wasn't, though, was she?"

He nods his head no. Of course, I was going to say something more sympathetic. Instead, the momentary truth rushes out. Of course I want him to be happy, but it stings to think of him with her. He looks at me and starts to laugh. It's that sweet, mirth-filled sort of laugh that was once so familiar to me.

"You haven't changed," he says with a smile.

"Lens, I miss you in the worst way."

"I miss you, too," he says so automatically that I know it's a lie

~

It seems that only a second passed between the strained talk in the café to the moment when we rush through the door of my apartment with our arms around one another. All those things that kept us apart have vanished along with my fears that he didn't miss me. Our feelings come pouring out in the way we hold and kiss each other, and I can think of nothing else but adoring Lens and making love to him.

The truth is that we cannot get close enough to one another. I need him inside me so badly that I reach for the zipper on his jeans as soon as we're inside the apartment. He pulls off my polka dot dress and unhooks my bra, and I free my hands so that I am able to quickly pull his periwinkle shirt over his head.

"I love you," he whispers, and I declare my love for him in the seconds between our kisses.

We kick off shoes and socks as our hands explore one another. We kiss as we somehow move our bodies into the bedroom, and I gently push him onto the bed. It has been so long since I've seen his body, and how beautiful he looks takes my breath away. In all the stages that we've been together, in this time and the other, I'm always madly attracted to him. His eyes are wide with desire, too, and I climb on top of him as he takes me in his arms.

I need to touch every part of his body, and I feel his hand between my legs. His touch makes me feel ecstatic and completely filled with longing. He slides off my panties, and I can't wait another moment. The desire is dizzying, and I must have him.

My legs are on either side of his hips, and I gently pull him into me. I feel pure bliss swirling and swelling. His low moans turn me on even more, and he grabs my hips to guide me as I call out his name. I feel the greatest thrill as he climaxes inside me. I kiss him deeply as I savor every second that we're together, then I find myself crawling into his arms with a contented sigh.

Chapter 61 ~ Darling

"How did we ever let anything come between us?" Lens asks. "You should know that I looked for you over and over again. I even looked you up online."

He has been by my side all day. Our reunion yesterday seems to be only the beginning, and the passion between us has been growing all day. We are giddy and happy, and we're not afraid to show it. We hold one another as we sit on the loveseat in my living room.

"Tell me something that makes you ashamed," Lens says as he looks at me in the most intense way, almost as though he's studying something that fascinates him.

"Why would I dare to do that?" I josh without even stopping to think about the words my mouth is forming.

"Because I've never been more embarrassed in my life. I've just basically admitted to stalking you. Come on here; comfort me!" he pleads, softening his eyes in a way that makes me want to kiss his long eyelashes as they beat down softly on his full cheeks.

"You shouldn't be," I say sweetly.

"You remember, don't you? Our past love?"

I am shocked beyond anything I'd ever imagined. Leonard places his hands on my shoulders as if to steady me, and he gently pulls me into his lap.

"You remember. You're echoing? Since when? All along? What?" I cry.

"We got married," he says. "I remember that."

"And the next one?"

"We were so happy together, and then one day you disappeared. A few hours later, I found myself waking up, and I was at that table with you…and Janet. I had no idea what was going on. I had no memory of Janet at all, but I remembered you. You left so quickly. I didn't have a clue about tracking you down. I tried to forget it all because it was so painful to be without you for so many years. Janet was such a comfort. I thought I'd be happy with her, but I wasn't."

"You chose her over me, though," I reason, "At least then, you chose her."

"I choose you," he says sharply. "I always will. I love you."

I am still not quite able to fully accept that Lens knows. I can share everything with him now. We can be together. How is it possible?

"You love me, too. I can tell. You're beyond obvious," Lens says with a gentle smile. "I love you."

Lens reaches down and pulls something out of his pocket. It's a CD that is designed to look like a miniature record album. I always used that sort of CD to make mixes for him.

"I recreated the mix CD you made for me after we first made love," he says.

"I've made a lot of mix CDs for you, but I didn't make one after we first did it," I reply, realizing too late that I've referred to making love more casually than he did.

"Come on. That memory of our other lives is something I'll always remember."

It dawns on me that he has memories of lives that we lived together that I don't have. I also have a recollection of an entire lifetime that I spent loving him that is unfamiliar to him. He offers to play the CD for me anyway, and I get up to turn on the stereo.

After I put on the CD, I sit back down, and he throws his arms around me. He kisses me before "Always" by Bon Jovi, the first track on the CD, even starts to play.

"This is incredible," I say when I come up for air. "We can finally be together with no secrets. There's nothing that can tear us apart."

He agrees by kissing me. As I kiss him, I feel so excited and turned on that I think I may just pass out. I can't believe that he's really here, and our truth can be fully expressed. I am in awe of him. His lips feel beautifully strong as they touch my own, and I feel a moan escape from deep inside. I hope he doesn't think that's weird. I wish that my insecurities would disappear, and they do for a moment as he kisses me deeply once again.

Chapter 62 ~ Sated

I'm running out of reasons to kill myself. That was the thought that I had, waiting on the pile of dirty restaurant linens, in the rain. I'm getting happier, so my suicidal daydreams are subsiding. Most people, when given good news, rejoice. I merely subtract the negative experiences from the positive ones. I hope to break even one day. Then maybe I'll never think of killing myself again. I don't make promises to myself, though. I'd hate to disappoint me.

There's not a doubt in my mind that Lens and I are soulmates. I never imagined that this is how things would be, but the shared love that we are building on with honesty now is too wonderful to ever deny.

Now we hang out as his place and make plans to marry again. Lens turns on his stereo and searches through the shelves of CDs in his room. I think of the past, which now seems to be only the future, and I consider how playlists will make those CD musical libraries so rare.

"Play me your favorite song?" I ask.

"I think that can be arranged."

He goes to the shelf right beside the stereo and quickly skips ahead as soon as he puts the CD in. As the opening notes of "Dreams Will Come" by Paul Brady enchant me, Lens tells me that he is more than a little in love with the song. He goes on about how it's infused with what he perceives to be the emotions of love and hope, and I find myself trying to listen to the song through the filter of his own perception. I'm wondering what memories he's had with the song.

"It's beautiful. How'd you find it? I've never heard of this album," I say as I pick up the album called *Trick or Treat*.

"Oh, you know," he shrugs. "What, may I ask, is your favorite tune?"

"No, no, no. Tell me! I want to know. Was it an old girlfriend?"

"Uh, no. Guess again, Miss Newman."

"You heard it as you walked around looking at the fine art of the Louvre on some overcast day in Paris?"

That makes him laugh, which turns the corners of my mouth up involuntarily.

"Have you actually ever been to a museum? I thought that was sort of how we met. You know, they don't play love songs at the Louvre."

We end up in fits of laughter, and I find myself collapsing in a giggle fit on his blue couch. He sits beside me, and we look into each other's eyes.

"I heard it on a soap opera," he finally confesses.

"There is no shame in watching soap operas. The politically correct word, though, is daytime dramas. Show some respect," I smile.

"Pardon me," he says.

It's amazing how casual our conversations become now that we have so much depth to our relationship. The mundane becomes magical when you're not fighting for each moment. I feel that maybe we have an infinite amount of moments, and that allows a sort of comfort that I'd never known.

Chapter 63 ~ Antidote

It's a beautiful autumn day, and I wear the necklace that my brother gave me so long ago. It has somehow made its way to me in all my lifetimes. It's a thing of permanence that I treasure.

I had to visit my parents' memorials alone, but Lens walks with me to visit Davey's grave. I feel weird being here. I've never been okay with the cemetery or the tombstone as being places where I can visit him. It feels foreign and false. I know that his body as I knew it may be buried, but I'm certain that what remains of his body is no more who he is than the dead skin cells that his body shed throughout his lifetime.

Although graveyards aren't scary to me, I dislike them just the same. After all, I know the true "self" of a person couldn't possibly be constrained by their remains in a grave. A body is just a shell of who we really are, in my opinion, and so it is this fact that leaves me without deep guilt for going so long without a visit to Davey's headstone.

I place flowers on my brother's grave along with a turquoise stone as a small way of saying thanks for the connection to him that the necklace provides. I also leave a note about what I've discovered about life and love since we were last together. I don't know if he would be proud of me, but I think maybe he will be if he can see the future I intend to build for myself.

"Good-bye, Davey," I manage to squeak, and there's nothing left to say.

I miss his rebellious spirit. He taught me to question authority. Leonard wraps an arm around me as we leave the cemetery. I know that I won't return there. I'll look for my brother elsewhere, in places where his spirit would thrive and find joy.

~

After we arrive back home, I sit on the bed I share with Lens and savor the crisp autumn breezes that flow through the open window. It's cool, yet just enough sunlight trickles in to make everything feel cozy. Lens walks into the bedroom, sits down beside me, and takes my hand in his. We're partners who have chosen to go through this life together, and we've been together for decades.

I never expected more than just individual joy, yet I've managed to fall in lasting love. More than that, Lens and I can be completely open and honest with one another in a way that we can't be with anyone else in the world. That helped our connection grow, and now it's stronger than ever.

Chapter 64 ~ The Letting Go

I am feeling enormously happy right now. You know, what I feel is a wow kind of happy. Things in my life are far from perfect. In so many ways I am lower and with fewer advantages than I've had in many other points in many lifetimes. Despite that, though, I find myself outrageously happy. Perhaps happiness is what comes with true wisdom.

I mourned for a long time when I found myself at another point in a time and place without Lens, and one in which he didn't remember me at all. The closeness that we shared for years when we could be completely and totally open with one another was worth any pain that I feel now, though, and I'm still able to live on the happiness I had then. There was such an abundance of it that it will overflow into many of my future years.

My journey through time isn't over. So now I'm within yet another echo. The awareness of all my lives are vivid and dear. I lost Mom, Dad, and Davey yet again. I couldn't stop it. I'll always try, though. I'll never give up on them. It hurts like hell that they are gone from me again, but I have reasons to hope that I will see them again. Not in this time, but time passes by so quickly. I love them enough to trust that I can let go now, because I'll try something new to save them next time. I'll find a way.

I am experiencing 1997 yet again, and it's even more charming this time around. As a present to myself for my "eighteenth" birthday, I've rented a small house right on the beach in Fairhope. I want the solitude. I need the time to think. I desire a day all to myself so that I can really sort out all these dreams I have on my mind.

First things first, though. I'm dancing on the beach. I throw my right leg up in the air, doing a half-split as the oncoming waves wash over me. I jump over the next wave and then start to waltz before I even realize what I'm doing.

This time, I am living with a bit of abandon. I eat what I want whenever I want, and I stop when I feel full or simply like I've had enough. I move as much as I can simply because I love to dance, and I revel in how my body feels in motion. I've stopped counting calories and conforming to some way of life that doesn't make me want to shout out loud about how much pleasure and joy I've felt in the day.

I still think of my first-ever memory in my original life. That memory of being beaten is far more vivid than I want it to be. It won't let go. My father seemed to delight in the beating of my tiny body. It also hurts that he bragged about it without repercussions. Others laughed along with him. The mirth that filled his voice sickens me to this day. At least when he was beating me, though, he was not hitting the animals that I loved.

In 1930, Bertrand Russell said to *Everyman* magazine, "When you think it is your duty to inflict pain, scrutinize your reasons closely."

The thing is, you don't have to be the one inflicting the pain to be evil. What still bugs me the most is that nobody did anything about the suffering I endured. When I imagine myself in that room when it happened, or as someone that he told, what I want to say is: *Protect her.*

I've never protected myself, though. Maybe that is why I go through all these echoes. Perhaps they are revisions. If they're other chances from God, I'm taking them more seriously now.

Things have not exactly been easy for me since I was little or even since that sad little May in my first life when I chose chocolate over death, but I have had lots of joy along the way. I am excited about many things on the horizon now. Oh, the joys we'd miss if we gave into the darkness that sometimes calls to very sensitive spirits.

I often think about the moment when I woke up as my thin, younger self during my first echo. I will try figure out what the connection is being thirty-seven and how I woke up in 1989. I will search for something more than the fractions of answers I find to the complete questions in my head. I will long to be able to make sense of the most essential knowledge of my life.

Chapter 65 ~ Savor the Zeal

I decide to go on a road trip to no place in particular. The idea is to drive until I find something worth stopping for, and I place no time limits on this road trip. I may drive forever and find a way to sustain the lifestyle as I go. I feel very little fear, and I am able to squash my old anxieties.

I drive a Corvette convertible with the windows down and the volume on my stereo turned up. I sing along to as many songs as I can. I perform "Bitch" my Meredith Brooks to my steering wheel as I accelerate up a mountainside in Tennessee, and I sing "Peaceful Easy Feeling" by the Eagles as I drive up the Pacific Coast Highway along the California coast. I leave private performances of "You Oughta Know," "Summer Nights," "Control," "Father Figure," "On My Own," and "Express Yourself" all over the country.

One day I feel compelled to stop the car when I come across a lavender field! I park and rush towards its beauty. When I reach it, I almost want to fling myself directly onto it all. Instead, I touch only the top of the lavender at the edge of the field. I feel it with my fingertips, then caress my own cheek. I want to savor how it feels for myself as I walk further into the field.

I am wearing a bright, pastel pink sundress. Its princess top hugs my body, while its long flowing skirt swishes a little as I walk. I slowly start to feel euphoric from my heart to my head. Then, as though it's expanding all over my body, I suddenly want to skip, so I do. I love being alone so I can give in to those sorts of impulses. I hold my arms out to my sides as I feel the wind blowing my long, curly hair. Savoring the moment and taking in my surroundings, I inhale deeply to fully take in the fragrance of the field.

I am older today that I've ever been, but I never felt younger in my whole life. For the first time, I know with absolute certainty that my body is my own. I can do whatever the hell I want to with my one and only beautiful body. I don't care what size it is. I just want to move it and love it and care for it.

Today I know that my life is my own. It came to me this morning as I soaked in a bubble bath. I inhaled in all the beauty I'd yet to experience, and I knew where I had to go. I also knew what I had to do. I knew that this was the day that my world was changing.

I feel the elation that had been denied my whole life, and I know what's coming. *I am a dancer.* I can't help it. It's what I feel to the very core of my being. I am a dancer, so I'm going to actually work at it and become the best dancer I can possibly be.

I started to tell one story, then I met someone who changed how I feel about everything in the world. So my story shifted, and I began again. I discovered me.

Chapter 66 ~ One for the Road

I know that Lens will be in the city, too, but I know that I can handle it if he doesn't remember. I will be okay. I trust that he will want to be with me again someday if it's God's plan, and I am able to let go of those unrealistic expectations that are so tempting.

I go to the museum once a week as a way of renewing my emotional energy and feeling a connection to the love I feel for Lens that has so defined the comfort I've found in life. I don't expect anything except the familiar joy I feel when I look at one of his paintings. The Met has three of them now, and I like gazing at them. I imagine how he felt creating them, and I wonder if he intended to make people feel quite the way that I feel when I look at them.

One winter day in 1999, I turn around and go to leave the museum. I am so surprised to see Lens there that I almost fall flat on my face. That would be typical of the old me, though, the one who denied her grace as a dancer.

I look at Lens again, and I can't deny that he is watching me. He and I are now face to face. I think: *Oh, please remember me.*

"Hello."

"Hello," he says. "What do you think of that piece there?"

"Oh, I love it. To tell you the truth, it's why I come here."

"For the artist?" he asks with a sly smile.

I don't know exactly why, but that's it. I know then that he's trying to let me know that he remembers, but he's scared, too.

"Lens," I whisper.

He nods, but he doesn't say anything. I think I've shocked him. He looks at my dance bag that I'm carrying.

"Need a hand?" he asks.

"Um, yeah, sure," I say as I gasp for breath.

"You've come from the dance studio."

I nod, and he looks at me with what seems to be pride. He's proud of me. He always thought I should follow my dreams.

"Are you happy?" I ask as he takes my hand.

In the end, that's all I wanted to know; it's all I truly wanted for him. Pure, unending, and unconditional love makes no demands.

So, how am I supposed to savor the *seconds* when they stretch out for an eternity?

Happiness is sustainable if you don't compromise who you really are. I believe that one person can make a big difference one step at a time. I believe that people are good at heart. I still believe in love and happily-ever-afters. I believe in turning it all around. I believe that dreams can come true. I believe that society's sense of right and wrong is extremely flawed, but I strive to help the world become a kinder place to exist.

When I make decisions, I consider how much of our lives are what we have created and chosen for ourselves. I was first suicidal as a child, and perhaps I will always be in danger of relapsing. If parts of your very self were formed partly from pain, it is hard to feel whole sometimes.

For now, I'm good, and I won't hide what I have to say ever again. I'm thankful to be alive in this exact moment. Whatever the future holds, oh how I love Lens. I adore this wild and wondrous world. I feel compelled to say a quick prayer of gratitude. As I open my eyes, I realize how deeply I love myself.

About the Author

Robin Raven is the human who once belonged to the greatest dog that ever lived. *Next Stop: Nina* is Robin's debut novel.

Born in Mobile, Alabama, Robin grew up in a nearby town called Saraland, and her hometown is a lovely place that still inspires her. As an adult, Ms. Raven has mostly lived in Los Angeles and New York City, so she also considers those cities to be home.

If she's not reading or writing, you can probably find Robin day-dreaming about adopting a rescue donkey. Delicious vegan food rocks her world. So does effective altruism. In addition to being an author, Robin has worked as a professional actress. She made her film debut opposite Charles Dutton in *The Third Nail*.

She blogs at RobinRaven.com.

Made in the USA
Lexington, KY
04 October 2015